WHAT WON'T DIE

ASHEA GOLDSON

GOLDWRITE PUBLISHING LLC

COVENANT TRIBE
M E D I A

Ashea Goldson/GoldWrite Publishing LLC
Covenant Tribe Media
An imprint of GoldWrite Publishing LLC
Metro Atlanta, GA/USA
www.GoldWritePublishing.com
www.Covenanttribemedia.faith
www.Covenanttribemedia.com

Publisher's Note: This is a work of fiction. Names, characters, places, and incidents are a product of the author's imagination. Locales and public names are sometimes used for atmospheric purposes. Any resemblance to actual people, living or dead, or to businesses, companies, events, institutions, or locales is completely coincidental.

ISBN: 978-1-7333188-7-7

Printed in the United States of America

DEDICATION

This book is dedicated to anyone who has experienced something so traumatic that you blamed God, lost hope, or turned your back on your faith, may you be caught up in the eternal grace and mercy of the ever loving Father and softly find your way back home.

(I Corinthians 13:8a Love never fails.)

ACKNOWLEDGMENTS

To my Lord and Savior Jesus Christ, without whom, I would have no gift of storytelling. I am honored to use what you have given me for Your glory. I thank you.

To my husband Don, with whom I've been blessed to spend the past thirty-seven years, for encouraging the endless stories that live in my head, for driving me to all of my writing functions, and for doing it all with a smile, I thank you. To my children and grandchildren for being the light of my life: Ana, Safy, Mall, Riah, Jam, Mari, Ari, Lani, Ky, and Zy, I thank you.

To my mom Janet, for being my constant cheerleader and a graceful woman of God, I thank you.

To my awesome extended family, church family, friends, colleagues, and students who have had any part in this book through reading, purchasing, marketing, reviewing, advising, praying, encouraging, or for bringing simple joy and laughter into my life while I was writing it, I cannot name all of you, but you certainly know who you are. I thank you.

To Pastor Murkison and Lady Val of VOFS for preaching the unapologetic Word of God and extending the immeasurable Love of God to me, I thank you.

To my supportive readers, for purchasing and reviewing this book, I thank you. You have made such a significant impact in my writing journey.

ONE

I've often thought that Harlem would have been an interesting place to die because it was such a special place to live; the contrast was inescapable. It was the kind of place that demanded attention. Everywhere I looked, there was life; children laughed, echoing as they jumped through knotted double dutch ropes, dunked basketballs through makeshift hoops, or frolicked in the cascading streams of open fire hydrants. The older women trudged through the crowds, with their adorning blue-gray wigs, determined and unyielding as they pulled their aluminum shopping carts behind them, filled with all they deemed necessary, including their dreams. Then the young progressives appeared as a testament to Harlem's ever-evolving spirit, purposefully tapping their designer shoes along the sidewalks, even if they were sneakers. They moved with hair flowing or making a statement, clutching leather backpacks and sleek briefcases, a manifestation of ambition and determination. In this urban symphony, every footstep became a note; every voice became a verse, as the city itself seemed to orchestrate so many lives. It even tried to manipulate mine.

There seemed to be a relentless rhythm in Harlem, humming with vitality, with its people moving on and off the streets, in and out of stone or brick buildings, talking and laughing, darting back and forth through traffic, expecting to live- not die. No matter how hard I tried not to hear them, I could not drown out the sounds of the cars and buses as they rolled over the potholes or the clinking of café dishes filled with fresh bagels and cups of espresso as the aroma wafted through the air. What probably seemed like the soundtrack of life to most, sounded like noise to me.

Yes, I observed the street vendors selling a variety of trinkets to unsuspecting pedestrians, eager to win them over with their NYC-branded hats and t-shirts, handbags with stories of their own, and handcrafted jewelry, whispering tales of the artisan's style. The streets were crowded, but I didn't mind. It was there in the crowds that I could hide every day, and no one would notice me. It was here, in the middle of one hundred and twenty-fifth street, that no one knew who I was or where I'd come from. It was here in the crowd that I could be anonymous.

Yet being invisible turned out to be hard work, and it all started the day I cut up my New York State driver's license, my social security card, and my American Express cards. I sat in front of the television with a bowl of raisin bran, refusing to get up for work. I stopped accepting any new clients, stopped paying the mortgage, and let the cable, power, gas, and water get turned off. I even let the bank pick up the Mercedes SUV and the Lexus. I ignored all of the phone calls, emails, visits, and heartfelt pleas from my friends and family. I covered all of my furniture in black satin. The people who claimed to care about me called it depression, but I called it my new reality. Finally, I disappeared from my two-story colonial home in Sands Point late one night, taking nothing with me except the clothes on my back, an oversized backpack, and what I held sacred in my pocket. That was how I ended up here in Harlem. I escaped, and I've been hiding out ever since.

It had all happened a little over two years ago. By the time mid-April came rushing in, spring had everything in bloom; I could hardly believe that it snowed just a few weeks ago. Yet, today, I felt the transformation; I stretched to greet the sunshine as it warmed my creamy brown skin. The brightness of the sunlight made me cringe and shield my eyes with a piece of cardboard. Who needed sunglasses anyway? It was amazing how simply you could live if you had to. In my typical native New Yorker fashion, I quickly climbed the steep concrete steps to the Home Again Women's Transitional Shelter. Before I hit the top step, I could hear Ms. Baptiste, the director, say, "You hungry, gal?" Ms. Baptiste's Caribbean accent was so mellow, but her voice always got my attention.

I looked up and nodded. "Yes, Ma'am?"

She stuck her head back inside the building.

Ms. Rosemarie Baptiste was the shelter director, a tall, thick Trinidadian woman with long, stringy, silver-gray locs and smooth dark chocolate skin; she was probably in her mid-sixties, although no one dared to ask her age and she never offered it. Her small, not-for-profit shelter housed thirty people, not including herself—a combination of women and children. To many, she was like the mother they never had. To me, she was a lifesaver; she lured me from a park bench when I was at my lowest point, and she brought me here. Although I found many excuses not to stay and even tried to sneak away at the beginning, I'd been here at the shelter ever since. Some people might even say I was stuck here. But they'd be wrong because I would be forced to leave soon. I'd already reached my second anniversary at the shelter and the end of my two-year maximum for The Uplift Program. Now I was just living out my time on the extension I'd been given.

Yet, nothing had changed for me and I certainly didn't feel uplifted. I didn't want to continue to be a burden to Ms. Baptiste though; I knew she'd try to find a loophole for me to stay. That was the kind of woman she was. So I'd made up my mind to leave before my deadline —to sneak away in the middle of the night—but this time to completely disappear forever. I had sixty days to make the pieces fit together. Sixty days.

Lately, I spent my days at the shelter, which was quite a different way of life for me. There was no privilege and no Prada- only hard work and accountability. There were three stories in this brownstone building and there were cedar wood floors throughout. We shared a common living room, kitchen, and dining room, which were all on the first floor. There was a huge playroom for the children in the finished basement area. Then there were our bedrooms on the second and third floors, complete with a twin-size bed and chest of drawers for each woman; roommates had to share a small closet. There were always at least two women assigned to a room along with bunkbeds for their kids, if they had any. Then there was old Mr. Williams, the red and gray-bearded, freckle-faced security guard from Mobile Alabama; he always had time to tell you a story, whether you wanted to hear it or not. It was his job to sit in the lobby by the front door, making sure that everyone checked in and out, and that no one missed the ten o'clock PM curfew. That was when Ms. Baptiste wanted everything locked down so she could go to bed to "rest her nerves," she'd say. However, old Mr. Williams was often found napping at his post in the middle of the day.

Most of the women there had children except for two older women, and my roommate Ashley and me, which was probably why she put us together for the past six months. I didn't mind as long as I had a clean and warm place to sleep, and I don't think Ashley did either. We each had our own cross to bear. She usually kept to herself, and so did I, except for the weekly group counseling sessions. It was there that I realized we had more in common than either of us realized at first. After getting to know a little of her story, I believed that we both had the same problem—life. The way that girl devoured drugs before Ms. Baptiste found her, she was lucky to be alive. As for me, I guess I was lucky too, but I still struggled to find a way to feel alive again.

Once I entered through the front door, I checked in with Mr. Williams in the small lobby.

He chuckled. "What are you cooking up tonight, Gabby?"

"Don't worry. I'll surprise you, Mr. Williams." I walked straight to the ladies' room to wash my hands; it was time for dinner duty.

I stood in front of the mirror and observed my face. At thirty-eight years old, my skin was still fairly smooth, which was surprising considering I used no age enhancing cosmetics lately-only cheap lotions. Yet, I could still see slight signs of aging around my almond-shaped eyes. Lately, they seemed sunken in and hollow due to a lack of sleep; bad memories haunted my dreams. My eyes looked like my father's, except that they weren't red and swollen with the effects of Johnny Walker Red. I ran my fingers through the newly grown strands of curly hair on my head before putting on the customary hairnet. I was almost bald a year ago, and that was by choice. *Who needed long hair anyway?* I remembered the day I put an electric razor to my head to shave off my brown, shoulder-length, golden-highlighted, silky layers of relaxed hair. Ms. Baptiste had been hysterical about the shaving. "Gal, don't ya know how many little black girls would kill for that hair?"

"Well they can have it," I'd responded.

Ernestine came into the bathroom and interrupted my thoughts. "I'd get out of the mirror if I was you," she said.

"Don't start with me today, Ernestine," I huffed.

That was Ernestine Henderson, a thirty five year-old corn-row queen. She could braid every style that was known to the culture, and that was her pride. Whether it was natural hair or weave, she had you covered. Around her neck, she boasted a snake tattoo—a cobra—and it fit her because she was venomous. Maybe her time in prison had hardened her. All I knew for sure was that she'd been known to start trouble, with me in particular. She liked to circle me and cut me with her eyes. But I refused to let her get to me because I had chores to do, and I didn't like messes. *Pull it together; fix it up, everything in its place.* So I simply walked away. Ernestine would have to wait.

After dinner duty, it was time to eat. There were three rows of tables, each seating ten people comfortably. And every evening, all the spaces were filled with women and children. A few of the women had mental health issues and had been thrown out of institutions for not having insurance. But Ms. Baptiste didn't mind working with people when she needed to. It was the kind of shelter that served as a temporary dwelling for some but served as a lifeline for others; for me, it was the latter.

As I collected the plates, Ernestine whispered, "Thanks, Ms. Uppity."

"Uppity?" I rolled my eyes and refrained from making a scene. If we argued, we'd both get our privileges taken away.

I didn't know where Ernestine got that *uppity* impression from because I tried my best to conceal my truth.

"You don't belong here, Gabby," she continued. "You're a fake."

"I'm more real than you," I spat out.

"You two, stop it right now," Ms. Baptiste scolded. "You're acting like children."

"Sorry," I whispered.

Ernestine smirked but said nothing.

"Don't forget that we have our annual street festival coming up next week. I need all of you to stay focused, invite some folks, and get us some help," Ms. Baptiste said, frowning. "It's really important that we have a real voice in the community, not waste time with this nonsense. I'm warning you all; get along, ladies!"

It sounded good, but I was not interested in having a voice. I only wanted to slip away into anonymity once the time was right again. After dinner, I tried to sneak away from Ms. Baptiste's prying eyes, but she cornered me in the kitchen.

"Gabby, have you invited your parents yet?'

"No, Ma'am. Not at all," I said.

"What ya' mean, not at all? What about your parents? I'm sure they'd like to come and support you." Ms. Baptiste spoke so fast that I initially had trouble understanding what she said. Whenever she was annoyed, her accent rose with heaviness in her throat and caused her to sound less clear.

I looked at her. "They don't really know where I am, and I'd kind of like it to stay that way."

"Gabby, you can't keep running forever." Ms. Baptiste looked me in the eyes. "Isn't that what we try to teach ya' here?"

I sighed. "I'm not running. I'm just surviving."

"Well, it's time to stop surviving and start thriving. I don't know all that ya' been through, 'cept the little you've told me, but I know ya' have a chance for a new start—a new life."

"I don't know about that, Ms. Baptiste. I haven't got much time left here and then it's over for me."

"Trust me. It ain't over till God says it's over." She patted me on the back. "His love never fails."

I mumbled, "Don't know about that..."

Ms. Baptiste put her finger under my chin to lift my head. "Call your parents. Trust me; it won't be so bad."

So I let her lead me to her office and reached for the phone. She looked at me curiously. I'd never had to use the house phone before.

"Sit down and act like ya' stayin a while." She smiled, showing her perfectly white teeth, before she left the room. I held the cordless phone in my hand, trembling before dialing the number. My shaky hands wiped the beads of sweat that accumulated on my forehead and upper lip.

I let the phone ring three times, and then I hung up abruptly when I heard his voice. That was it. I wouldn't call again. I left her office, closed the door behind me, and climbed the stairs to my bedroom the same as any other night. *Why can't I just say something? What is wrong with me?*

I reached the top of the stairs, carrying my shoes in my hands, and then turned the corner leading to my room. Luckily, Ms. Baptiste's bedroom was at the end of the hall. When I entered my room, the first thing I noticed was that my roommate Ashley wasn't there for some reason. I looked up at the wall clock. She'd always check in by nine thirty and not a minute later, so not seeing her sitting at her desk was unusual. She was studying to be a CNA, a certified nurse's assistant, and she wanted to graduate before her next birthday. Whenever Ms. Baptiste asked me what I wanted to study during my time in the Uplift Program, I didn't answer. I never told her what I used to do. And I surely didn't want to learn anything new; learning wasn't my problem. Life had already taught me enough.

For the past three months, I shared a room with Ashley Claremont, who was originally from Staten Island, but whose family had moved to Manhattan once they'd made it. She was twenty-six years old, tall and shapely, with long, silky, brownish blonde hair and bright, bluish gray eyes. When I first laid eyes on her, I wondered what problems someone as beautiful as she was could possibly have. That was before she described her bout with meth and heroin and the toll it had taken on her soul. After examining her more closely and seeing the tracks on her arms, I also realized how the drugs had ravaged her young body; so much for beauty solving everything. I really wanted to help her, but I didn't know where to start. I glanced up at the clock again, confirming that Ashley was officially out past curfew.

Needing a distraction, I reached into my chest of drawers and took out the stack of tickets for the festival. I neatly placed them into my backpack. *Everything in its place.* Maybe Ms. Baptiste was right. Maybe the festival was just what I needed to take my mind off things. Tomorrow would already be difficult, but I hoped I could hold it together.

CHAPTER
TWO

There I was, choking back tears on what would've been *his* birthday, when I should've been celebrating and loving. But that had all been stolen from me. There I sat on the steps of The Harry Belafonte 115th Street Library, with its lackluster metal shelves piled high with stories when I couldn't even face my own. And there I was, sitting among city dwellers, pretending to be human, pretending to be more than bones and flesh. Yet, despite my deep grief, I heard them coming up the steps. I heard their playful voices and their mocking tones. Then, the shadows stood in my sunlight.

The first voice was gruff. "Hey, bag lady, what you doin' here?"

I looked up from my book just enough to scope out the scene, but I didn't answer. A group of four teenagers, all wearing dark-colored hoodies, surrounded me. Wasn't it too hot to be wearing hoodies? They all appeared to be taller than my five-foot, seven-inch frame. My first thought was that these kids should be in school, but after a moment, I realized that it was Saturday. One day had melted into another lately.

One of the boys pointed at me. "Haven't I seen you on the park benches 'round here?"

The second one chimed in, "Nah, I know her too. It's one of those cray crays from that shelter down on 125th Street."

"She's the one that walks around with all the bags," the third one said, chuckling.

I could feel my heart beating faster. It was true. I used to walk around with my bags clutched closely to my body because they were the only possessions I had left. Now, I'd limited them to one backpack. *How dare they?*

"Ugh, look at 'dem shoes," the first one said.

Then, the second one held out his hand for a fist bump. "I keep it one hundred. They're fire, Son." He started giggling uncontrollably.

"Yeah, she's got the drip," the third one mocked.

"Nah, man, she got it from the dumpster," the first one smirked, bending over with laughter.

The second one agreed, "No cap."

Now, that was it; I may have looked like a hot mess with my mismatched, non-fitting clothing, but at least my clothes were clean, and I bathed every day at the shelter, so I knew I didn't stink. My eyes narrowed in on them. *And who were they to talk with their tacky sneakers and sagging pants?* Surprisingly enough, something inside wouldn't let me answer them. I didn't know why I hadn't spat out the many nasty comebacks that were running through my mind. Oh yes, I had my mother's mouth, and Sadie, the queen of neck rolling, didn't take no junk. But there was something about this day in particular that had me feeling vulnerable. I reached into my pocket and squeezed the shiny object that kept me stable.

Instead of speaking, I looked directly at the fourth boy. His eyes seemed to see right through me; there was something eerie in his stare. He stood apart from the others and said, "Yo man, let's just go. We ain't got to pick on a homeless lady."

The first boy pointed to the fourth, still snickering. "I should've known you'd be a scary kid."

"Nah, you're just doing' too much; that's all." The fourth boy shrugged his shoulders.

"Aww, he's just soft, man," the second one said. "I shoulda known the mama's boy wouldn't say anything anyway."

They all started to giggle.

"Or maybe he's just got something more important to do," a deep-voiced stranger interjected as he took the last two steps and stood towering over the fourth boy.

Immediately, the kids scattered like ants under a heavy rain.

"I'm sorry." The stranger looked into my eyes. "Are you okay?"

"I can take care of myself; thank you." The last thing I needed was someone else's pity.

I grabbed my belongings, quickly ran up the steps, and into the library. After finding an empty seat, I was able to open my book again.

I'd waited for my favorite author's latest release to come in for weeks; there was something about a good mystery. I tried to get back into the story, to put the incident behind me but I was still trembling. A tear forced its way down my cheeks. I couldn't believe I was still so shaken up by those kids. Was I angry because they were so mean, or was I angry with myself for putting myself in this situation? If I dressed nicer, would I deserve to be treated better? I knew that wasn't true. If I appeared smarter, would they have tried me like they did? I couldn't believe I'd stood there like a fool and let them get to me. There was a time when I would've swallowed them up with my three hundred dollars an hour words. There was a time when my words were some of the highest-paid ones in the city. I shook my head in self-disgust. I was weaker today than usual; his birthday always had this effect on me.

Seconds later, I heard footsteps come up behind me. When I looked up, I saw the fourth boy standing next to me. I immediately stood up. "Are you following me?"

The boy said, "Oh uh no... I...uh..."

"You've got something to say?"

"Yeah." He kneeled down next to me. "Sorry about those guys being stupid before... I."

I squinted. "You're sorry?"

He stood up, then extended his balled-up fist towards me for a fist bump but I looked at this hand like it was poison.

After seeing the way I was looking him up and down, he quickly withdrew his hand. "Anyway, I'm Caleb, and I'm... uh real sorry."

I was confused. *Maybe it's a trick.* I looked around. There were no other boys. "Well… I'm Gabby- Ms. Gabby to you."

"We cool, Ms. Gabby?" He dusted off his pants.

"Whatever." I stood up and put my finger in his face. "Don't you ever go along with fools like that again when you know they're doing something wrong. Those wannabe thugs are not the kind of friends you need to have."

"Yes, Ma'am," he agreed. "They ain't really my…"

"They ain't?"

"I mean, they're not really my… I'm really just here to work on a speech." He took a piece of paper out of his pocket and offered it to me.

I snatched it from him. "Oh?" I was always a sucker for a good speech. "What kind of speech?"

He kept his head down. "I've been chosen to deliver a youth address at a fundraising dinner for Senator Kenneth Dawson."

My eyes opened wide. "Senator Dawson, huh?" I skimmed the paper and then handed it back to him. "Sounds like some honor."

"I guess," Caleb said, looking down at the floor.

"You guess?" I asked curiously, "How old are you?"

"Sixteen."

All of a sudden, there seemed to be less oxygen in the room. Once again, I reached into my pocket and squeezed.

Then the tall stranger appeared again with a basketball in one hand. "Sorry to bother you again, but I just wanted to make sure that Caleb has made things right with you. I'm his science teacher and mentor."

Not him again. "Are you a stalker?

"This is Ms. Gabby," Caleb said.

"Nice to meet you, Ms. Gabby. I'm Devin Ramos. You can call me Devin." He offered his hand, but I just rolled my eyes.

For the first time, I noticed that the stranger, Caleb's teacher had a warm golden complexion, dark brown hair, and thick-framed glasses. He was sporting a pair of fitted faded denim jeans and worn-out leather cowboy boots. *Who still wears boots this time of year?* His plain blue t-shirt clung to his muscular chest, although I could see nasty, fresh sweat stains. He looked to be over six feet tall and he had a sturdy build, broad shoulders, and a wide torso. In fact, he looked a little more like a construction worker than a teacher. All of the teachers I've ever had were either scrawny or overweight. He was neither.

Devin squinted as he looked me up and down.

I wasn't a fan of how he was looking at me, but I tried to mask my discomfort. *Don't stare at me, brother.* "Well, this kid has tried to make things right, but if you're his mentor, it seems like you're responsible for this unacceptable behavior."

Devin chuckled. "Now wait a minute. Are you saying this is my fault?"

I put my hands on my hips, something I hadn't done in a while. "I'm saying that your mentoring is off."

"Caleb is a good kid," Devin said.

"Well, your *good kid* needs to stop hanging around with knuckleheads," I spat out.

"You're right about that, and I've told him..."

"I don't need you to tell me that I'm right. Just handle your business, Mr. uh, science teacher mentor."

"Ma'am, I'm just trying to..."

Then I backed up. "Who are you calling, ma'am?"

"I'm sorry. You're probably too young to be called that."

I put up my hand. "You've got no right to try to figure out my age either."

"Again, I'm sorry, and I see that we're not going to agree no matter what, so Caleb, I'll meet you outside." Devin shook his head and threw up his empty hand, while balancing the basketball in the other. He headed towards the exit. "Have a good day."

I watched him walk out. What was a grown man doing bringing a basketball to a library anyway? *Mentor indeed.* I looked at the boy. "You might as well go on with him. Your teacher is rude, presumptuous, and..."

"He didn't mean anything by it. He's just..."

"He's just out of line," I continued.

Flustered, I could feel a migraine coming on. I looked at the books in front of me. *Pull it together; fix it up, everything in its place.* Tears of rage were filling up behind my eyelids. As I moved my bag, the stack of raffle tickets fell to the floor. "Oh no," I said, squatting down to pick them up.

"I'll help." Caleb helped me pick up the scattered tickets, one by one.

"Well, if you're going to help, at least do it properly, I said, taking one from his hand and placing it atop the pile. "Place them face up."

As Caleb placed the last of the tickets on the table, he picked up the flyer that went along with them. "Wow, how can I get in on this raffle?"

"Excuse me?"

"This festival that's coming up, this flyer says they will be raffling off a Play Station Five."

"So?"

"So I want one. My mom said she can't afford this new one right now, but if I could win one…"

I looked at him long and hard to see if he was just playing games. "The Home Again Women's Transitional Shelter, where I'm staying, is having its annual street festival, and those who attend will have a chance to win the raffle. It's kind of like a block party; nothing fancy like the senator's banquet, but we've all got to sell these tickets."

Caleb started digging into his pockets. "But how much are they?"

"Five dollars each. But you must bring a parent with you. No exceptions."

Caleb pulled out two crisp five-dollar bills. "Okay, cool. I'll take two."

After we'd made the exchange, he said, "See you at the festival."

"Whatever," I smirked. "You, stay out of trouble."

He made a quick dance move before backing out of the door. "I will."

I shook my head, not believing his antics. He reminded me of better days but I refused to let him see me smile.

As I slipped back into my seat, I remembered Ms. Baptiste's words. She'd practically begged all of the shelter residents to sell tickets to the festival. Maybe she'd get off my back since I'd at least sold two. Otherwise, I'd probably have to make that phone call again, and I didn't dare to think where that might lead.

THREE

DEVIN

It was late Sunday afternoon at Morningside Park. It was one of the more interesting parks in the city, filled with personality. There was its raw beauty with its shimmering lake and naturally green landscape, but then there were the needs of the surrounding neighborhood and the poverty-influenced crimes that lurked about. And just when it seemed as if the park should be feared rather than revered, one could look up to the top of the steps and fix their eyes on Columbia University, perhaps a beacon of hope. Then, one could know that, fair or not, life could be good. Devin took all of this in because he loved Harlem all day long, and nothing could change his mind. Still, the sun was bright, and today, the living was easy.

After an hour of helping Caleb with his assignment, Devin and Caleb ended up on the basketball court, playing around as they occasionally did. It was Caleb's idea to meet at the park, so Devin assumed he wanted to have a little recreation time afterwards. After all, Caleb's father lived in Chicago and seemed to have few opportunities to spend with him. Admittedly, Devin enjoyed taking up the slack. So Devin looked at his watch, and then threw the basketball to Caleb. Caleb caught it and threw it straight into the hoop.

"Yesss!" Caleb hollered.

They gave each other a high five as they finished up their quick game.

"Great game, buddy," Devin said, throwing a towel around his neck. Both of them fell onto the wooden park bench, exhausted. Perspiration glistened on their faces. "Well, I'm glad you've finished the important points for your speech."

Caleb gathered his books and placed them in his book bag. "I sure appreciate the help. Writing just ain't my thing."

"Isn't your thing," Devin corrected. "Don't worry, you've got a lot of cool ideas; you should be confident in your ability."

"I hope I don't get nervous tonight, though."

"I'm sure your presentation will be the highlight of the event," Devin said.

"Thanks, Mr. D.," Caleb nodded. "I wish you could be there."

"Not for a one thousand dollar ticket fundraiser. Not on a science teacher's salary." Devin threw his head back and laughed.

"Right." Caleb laughed, too. "Anyway, thanks again."

Devin gave him a firm pat on the back. "My thanks will be seeing you graduate with honors next year and going on to college."

Caleb stopped smiling. "I almost forgot. I wanted to ask you a favor."

Devin dribbled the basketball in front of him. "Sure. What is it?"

"So remember that homeless lady at the library yesterday?"

"Yeah, how could I forget? What about her?"

"So she was selling raffle tickets for a street festival fundraiser …"

"Okay?"

"So I bought a ticket so I can have a chance to win the PlayStation Five."

Devin smiled. "Oh, PlayStation Five. I see…"

"Man, I hope I win."

Devin chuckled. "Well, it's possible, but what's the problem?"

"The problem is that I need an adult to go with me, and my mom has to work late that day." Caleb hands the ticket to Devin.

Devin read the ticket. "A street festival, huh?"

"Yes, sir."

"Sounds like a block party to me." Devin smiled. "Okay, I can do that. I don't think Ms. Uh… Gabby will be happy to see me, but I guess I can manage to avoid her."

"Thanks, Mr. D."

"No problem." Devin reached into his pocket. "How much do I owe you for the ticket?"

Caleb held up five fingers, and Devin stuffed a five into the boy's hand.

Devin felt more than eager to help because his schedule was almost empty after attending the early morning service at his church. At forty-nine years old, besides ushering in his church two Sundays a month or grading papers alone in his studio apartment, he didn't look forward to doing anything. Sure, he'd sometimes shoot a few hoops with his friend from college, Simon, but that wasn't enough anymore. Even working out at the gym was getting lame. He wasn't sure what it would take to make him happy.

Caleb snapped his fingers. "Mr. D, are you alright?"

"Sure," Devin answered with certainty, but underneath it all, he felt defeated.

He looked at Caleb, and for a moment, he wished he had a son like him. He knew that he shouldn't have spent his younger years chasing women. Perhaps he should have settled down with one of them instead; he could have had a child. He could have been staring into the face of his own child right now instead of this teenage boy who already had parents of his own. He wondered if he was being selfish for thinking that way, for wanting a child of his own. It was a little late, but he wanted it just the same. He shook his head as he decided that he would have to make changes.

What a day it had turned out to be-early morning worship at his church in Brooklyn, one long tutoring session at the park with Caleb, and then a quick stop at the Whole Foods store. Devin walked into his apartment and surveyed the mess. For a bachelor's pad, it wasn't the worst in the world, but it wasn't exactly neat either. Devin walked into the tiny kitchen area and placed his two shopping bags onto the sink. He pulled out the pack of sliced turkey, mayonnaise, mustard, a head of romaine lettuce and juicy red tomatoes. He looked at the chili peppers, red vinegar and olive oil. After he'd put all of those items away, he continued to pull out the peanut butter, the whole wheat bread, orange juice, apples, bananas, celery, six cans of tuna, one bag of hot Cheetos, three bottles of PowerAde, and fresh kale. Tomorrow he would make himself a green smoothie but not tonight. He thought about ordering pizza, then looked at his stomach and decided against it. So he fixed himself a sub sandwich instead, complete with all of the extra fixings that he liked. It was an art he'd picked up from living in the frat house during college; he couldn't cook but he could make a mean sandwich. When he was done, he wiped his mouth, drank a bottle of PowerAde, and began to yawn. Stretching, he walked the few feet over to the sofa bed and pulled it out for the night.

Devin stood next to his full size sofa bed and pulled his shirt over his head. He pulled off his jeans, and then emptied the contents of his pockets onto the bed before going into his bathroom which was barely as big as a closet. Within minutes, he had immersed himself in the cool waters of his new shower head. It was a little something he'd treated himself to after his landlord refused to fix the old one. He shook his head under the spray as he considered his little studio apartment. It was too expensive, too small, and too old, but it was clean, rent controlled, and it was all his.

By the time he stepped out of the shower, he wrapped a cotton towel around his waist. He sat on the bed next to the pile of belongings he'd emptied there. His library card caught his eye and he immediately remembered the boy, Caleb. Devin smiled, enjoying the thought of helping him because he had an authentic passion for working with youth. Oddly enough, the face of that homeless woman he'd met at the library, popped into his head also. Now she was another story altogether.

He recalled how odd she was, quirky even, but she had beautiful brown eyes. She also had a sort of a hidden cuteness camouflaged by baggy clothes, void of any style. Then he chuckled at how she'd exploded on him repeatedly, like rapid fire. She didn't even allow him a chance to explain himself properly. After they'd left the library, Caleb told him that she lived at the homeless shelter, but he'd never met any homeless person quite like her before. It was almost like something was missing in her introduction. There was something mysterious about her but he couldn't pinpoint exactly what it was. He shoved his library card back into his wallet.

Just then the phone rang and he leaned across the bed to answer it. "Hello."

"Hi, stranger." It was Catherine. He recognized her sultry voice.

"Oh, hi Catherine." Devin bit his lip in resignation.

"Well, you don't sound excited to hear from me," Catherine teased.

Devin paced his bedroom floor. "No, it's not that. It's always good to hear from you. It's just that…"

"Oh, did I catch you at a bad time?"

Devin paused, desperately looking around the room for something to hold onto.

"Actually, I just came out of the shower and I was about to get some work done," he said, looking at the pile of papers on his side table.

"I'm sorry. I'll let you get back to it then," she said.

"No, it's okay." He put his hand up to his forehead. "Did you want something?"

"No, just checking on you since I hadn't heard from you in a while."

Devin held the phone close to his ear but was silent. He'd only taken her out to lunch once but it was possibly one of the biggest mistakes of his life. She wouldn't stop harassing him.

Devin scratched his head. "I'm sorry but I've just been really…uh busy with work…"

"Work is good but not without a social life."

"Story of my life. All work and no play," Devin said.

"You've got to take some time for yourself." Catherine giggled. "If you're anything like me, you're not getting any younger."

That was a joke. He was old enough to know that hooking up with her would mean trouble for him. "I'll make some time soon but right now I'm so involved with my students and making use of my doctoral studies that I hardly have time for anything else."

"That's right; you did just finish your program didn't you? Congrats!"

"Thanks. But with that being said, I've been very busy." He shook his head. "Too busy."

There seemed to be another long pause. "I understand. Well, I guess I'll see you at work tomorrow."

Devin ended the call with a quick goodbye and a long sigh.

How did he get himself into this? Catherine was Devin's colleague, one of the guidance counselors at the high school where he worked. She was only twenty seven years old and quite attractive. She had a nice figure and she wore tight fitted skirt suits to show off her shapely legs. She had dark reddish brown hair, dreamy eyes, and fake eyelashes. He wasn't really sure why he wasn't interested in her because she was surely interested in him, but he just wasn't. Maybe it was because of the countless failed relationships with women who seemed just like her. Perhaps he needed something different.

Devin threw his towel aside, put on his gray pajama pants and proceeded to shave. He then stared at himself in the mirror as he applied his after shave lotion. Once again his electric razor had assaulted him. For once he would have liked to get a smooth cut without being injured. He touched the spot that was bleeding and put pressure on it with his hand. He'd not only shaved his face but he'd trimmed his hair also. He'd made it so even that his grandfather, who had owned a barbershop back in the sixties, would have been proud of him. He looked from side to side, noticing the small patch of gray hair. He figured there was nothing he could do about that since his age was catching up with him. At a second glance, he realized that he didn't care for his profile either. His forehead was a little too big, and his hair was a little too straight, a trait he'd picked up from his half- Latina mother. He thought that maybe a beard was in order. Maybe that would make him look more distinguished; he did want more respect in his field. But the thing he really wanted more than anything, more than his career, was a wife. He'd admitted it to himself.

After all of his foolish shenanigans, he finally wanted a wife. He'd never been married before but he'd come pretty close once many years ago. The trauma of his fiancé leaving him for the glamour of Hollywood kept him from trusting for so long. But now he was convinced that it was time to try again. He just had to find the right woman. He knew he needed God's help with that task. He wasn't sure if she would come from his workplace, his church, or from his gym, but he knew that he needed a good one. He gave himself one more glance in the mirror and smiled. After patting himself on the head, he decided that he didn't look so bad for a nearly fifty year old man. Maybe, just maybe he would be able to find a mate, after all.

Devin went to lie down in his bed, grabbed his Bible off of the nightstand, read his usual two chapters, and whispered a short prayer. Then he took off his glasses and pulled the covers over his head. He didn't feel like grading papers or watching television. He didn't feel like doing anything at all; he was lonely.

He could hear the breeze blowing against his window pane and knew that a spring storm was brewing. Devin turned sideways so he could be more comfortable. At that moment he heard his bell ring. He looked at the clock, and seeing that it was almost midnight, wondered who it could be.

Unable to locate his slippers in the dark, he stumbled over to the door barefooted. As he looked through the peephole, he saw Caleb's face. He unlatched the door.

"What are you doing here so late?" Devin leaned partially into the hallway.

Caleb was dressed in a navy blue two piece suit. "I'm sorry, Mr. D, but I just had to say thanks again for all your help."

Devin rubbed his weary eyes. "The speech went well?"

"I killed it, Mr. D." Caleb held out his fist.

"Good for you, Caleb." Devin gave him a fist bump.

"And I met the senator's daughter too; she was hot."

Devin opened his mouth wide, and then playfully slapped him on the back of his neck. "Hey, you're the man."

"I think so," Caleb said, smoothing his budding mustache."

"Well, you'd better get home now."

"Right, my mom is outside waiting. I begged her to stop here." Caleb couldn't stop rocking with excitement.

"I'll see you in class tomorrow," Devin said. "Congratulations again."

"Thanks, Mr. D."

Devin closed the door behind Caleb with a sense of pure satisfaction. It seemed as if all of his sacrifices were paying off one way or another. Before he could walk away from the door, he heard Caleb knock again lightly. He snatched open the door.

Caleb swayed back and forth. "Sorry, but I forgot to tell you the most important part."

"What's that?"

Caleb did a little dance in the hallway. "I'm going out with the senator's daughter real soon."

"Good for you, kid. "Then Devin thought about it for a moment. "Be careful."

"Night, Mr. D."

As Devin shut the door for the final time, his mood had changed. Something inside of him would not let him be at ease. Delivering a speech was one thing but he couldn't help but to wonder if dating the senator's daughter was such a good idea.

FOUR

After a night of lucid dreams, I woke up to the reality that I was still alone. As I sat up in my donated twin sized bed, I remembered what I already knew; no amount of pain or grief could bring *them* back. Nothing could erase the emptiness of the last two years. I glanced over at my roommate's disheveled covers and wondered where she was. *Did Ashley even come home last night?* Immediately, I placed my feet onto the cold hardwood floor. I never did like cold hardwood and thankfully, Ms. Baptiste found it suitable to give each of us a pair of house slippers at the start of each winter. I walked over to the bathroom and slipped inside quietly. After washing the crust of tears from the rim of my tired eyes, I peeled off my bed clothes and plunged into the shower. As I climbed into the cold stall, the warm water felt soothing against my skin. I'd always liked the feel of a hot bubble bath but under the circumstances, a bath tub was a luxury I didn't dare think of anymore. There were no Chanel shower gels here either, just a plain white bar of good old fashioned Ivory soap. *Maybe this will help me feel human again.*

Sunday morning at the shelter was much like any other day except that Ms. Rosemarie Baptiste made a big deal about going to church. It seemed as if it was the highlight of her week. She would put on her finest cotton dress, pin her locks up underneath a big straw hat, and put on a pair of shiny pumps; no one could tell her she didn't look good. And for a woman her age, she did. Then she'd walk up and down the stairs, clicking her heels, and hollering instructions as she went. "Jesus is a healer," she'd say, "Oh, yes," referring to her ovarian cancer that had been in remission for the past ten years. Sometimes on Sundays Ms. Baptiste would take a few of the women with her, whoever she'd managed to convince for that particular week. They'd go with her and whether or not they were sincere, they'd all come back happier than they were when they left. Me, being the born again skeptic that I was, was never fooled.

When I came out of the bathroom, I went straight to the window to watch, what I referred to, as the Home Again parade. I stood at my window, behind the pastel blue curtains, peeking out at Ms. Baptiste who wore her emerald green maxi dress. She left with three other women and four young children. I smiled because despite their circumstances, they all looked their best. Ms. Marilyn, the older woman from two rooms down, had hot curled the women's hair and Ernestine had braided their daughter's hair as well. Mr. Williams had given the two baby boys haircuts also. I laughed to myself as I watched them follow Ms. Baptiste like she was royalty.

Then I glanced over at Ashley. She was sitting on her bed clipping her toenails. I sat down on my own bed and looked down at my own questionable looking toes with disgust. *When had she snuck in?*

Ashley whispered, "I'm sure you heard already."

I never looked up at her. "Heard what?"

"I didn't make it back on time," she explained.

"I noticed that." I paid her little attention.

"I ended up hanging out with a friend too long and next thing I knew it was ten o' clock and believe me, I was nowhere near Harlem."

I peered over at her. "Where were you?"

"Way up in the Bronx at 149th street," she answered, trying to avoid eye contact.

I already knew what that meant so I just nodded. The South Bronx was no place for her to be hanging out at night.

"Ms. Baptiste is tripping though so I won't get my weekend visit," Ashley huffed.

"Sorry, but she's probably just worried that you're using again." I waited for her reaction.

Ashley shrugged her shoulders. "I guess." She frowned.

I finally stood up and walked in front of her, forcing her to look at me. "You're not *using* again are you?"

She darted her eyes around the room, nervously. "Course not. You think I'm stupid?"

I remembered hearing those words so many times before. Like the time Ms. Baptiste tracked Ashley down at her old neighborhood drug house and dragged her back to rehab. Or the time she disappeared for two whole days, only to be brought back by a male stranger, "high as the clouds," Ms. Baptiste had described.

I'm not stupid either. "Nobody said anything about being stupid." That was all I had to say to her. She'd been coached, coaxed, counseled, and detoxed. She'd been in multiple treatment centers across New York City. Ashley's own parents had all but given up on her when Ms. Baptiste brought her in; she claimed that the only thing left to do was to pray, then trust that God would handle it. But I didn't do either of *those things* anymore.

As far as I was concerned they were on their own. "So you lost your visitation privileges?"

"Yep." Ashley pulled out bubble gum from her mouth, wrapped it around her finger, then stuck it back in.

"There are worse problems to have." I wasn't in the mood to hear her complain. I had enough problems of my own. *His* birthday was yesterday and the hole in my heart seemed to just keep getting bigger. And after two years in the Uplift Program, although I still had a warm bed, that security would run out as soon as my sixty day extension did.

"Before I came here, I was in a really abusive relationship. I was living with a guy who beat the crap out of me every single day." Ashley looked down. "You're right; this ain't such a bad place."

Before I could help myself I had gone over to give her a quick hug.

Ashley stood up and swung her purse onto her shoulder, dropping what looked like a small sandwich bag full of marijuana onto the floor. "Oh, I'm so clumsy."

"I can see that." I stared at the bag.

Ashley stooped down to pick it up. "Look, it's not what it looks like."

"Okay, I'll play your game. What do *you* think it looks like?"

"Come on; it's just weed and-" Ashley quickly stuffed it into her purse. "It doesn't even belong to me…"

I shook my head. "You don't owe me any explanation."

"Okay-cool." Ashley started towards the door.

 I paused and then added, "But don't you owe one to yourself?"

"Aw man, here we go."

"I'm not trying to lecture you, Ashley, but I'm going to say that I see us headed down the same road."

Ashley sucked her teeth, and then turned around. "What *road* are you talking about?"

"I see you and me on a dangerous road, except I think maybe you might want to reconsider."

"Humph. Ain't nobody out here trying to get hurt. I just want to have a little fun. I've been good ever since I left rehab."

I shot her a look.

Ashley smirked, "Okay, since I left rehab the last time."

"Maybe you need help so you can make better choices."

"Maybe you need help minding your business." Ashley stood with her arms folded, rolling her eyes up to the ceiling. "Am I free to go now, Mother, or should I say Warden?"

It was true that I was no one's mother. "Do what you want," I snapped.

After hearing those words she was gone.

I listened for the sound of the door slamming, then watched her from the window. Since I'd been living here, window watching had become a habit of mine. Like television, it was a safer way to experience life, a more honest one too. No one hid from the window watchers, especially on 125th street; perhaps, that was because no one expected to be watched. But up high you could see and hear all kinds of things: people's true expressions, arguments, and sometimes if you were mindful, you'd see the secrets of one's heart.

Ashley crossed the street, looked both ways, and then took off running toward the train station. That told me that she was afraid of something. Not sure of what to think, I shook my head. *That girl's in trouble.*

I threw on a pair of navy blue sweatpants with a white t-shirt, grabbed my backpack and set out to fulfill my promise.

"Hey, where are you going?" someone asked but I didn't recognize the voice so I didn't stop to see who it was. Instead, I bounded down the front steps, then kept walking past people, buildings and cars until I reached the subway station. I even passed by a local church, shutting my mind and heart against it as I walked. *Never again will I believe.*

I was finally going home. Minutes later I was running down the subway's staircase, paying my fare, and standing near the tracks. I leaned over a bit to see if a train was coming, careful not to stand too close to the edge. There was always something happening underground. Before long, the train approached in its entire noisy splendor. I stepped back a few inches. Someone tapped me on the shoulder. I turned to face the culprit with my wrath but it was just a little old man selling umbrellas. They were cuter than the plain black one I already had but since I was no longer interested in style, I shook my head to indicate that I didn't want one. Besides I didn't have any money to waste, just a Metro card that would allow me to get to my destination and back. Besides, I'd been saving up for the day I had to depart The Home Again Women's Transitional Shelter. I couldn't waste money on frivolous things. Finally, the train pulled into its station and I winced as the doors opened, then shut.

The ride to Brooklyn was as comfortable as it had always been, although I hadn't traveled this way for quite some time. All of the stops, announced by the conductor became a blur. I watched the stops go by, Bay Parkway, 25th Avenue, then Bay 50th Street. I wondered if *they* would be happy to see me when I got there. I stood by the door as they opened, waiting to step onto the platform; yet at the last minute, I decided not to and stepped away from the closing doors. Instead of getting off at Bay 50th, I decided to ride the train to the next and final stop-Coney Island.

When I stepped off of the train, I felt a sense of relief. Growing up here in Brooklyn, and ironically, just a train stop away, Coney Island , had always been one of my favorite places. I could smell the Atlantic Ocean as I quickly walked up Stillwell Avenue the few blocks to Brighton Beach. Once I reached the boardwalk, I took off my sneakers and walked awkwardly through the sand. As I neared the shore, I bent down to pick up a sea shell. I sniffed it, then put it to my ear to hear the waves. I stared out at the waves, remembering coming here with my parents and brother when I was a little girl. Then I recalled the first time I drove down here with my husband and son. Already a water freak, my husband Barry loved the beach and our son Teshaun was most excited about what used to be Astroland Fun Park; it was now Luna Amusement Park since new management took over. Although it was not fully open for the season yet, it was open on the weekends in April and May. I could hear the screams of people on the thrill rides. Surprised that *the* Cyclone was still running, I smiled. It was truly the best roller coaster of all time and I'd been on quite a few.

Barry and I used to argue over that point often. I explained to him that the iconic ride on the Cyclone's rickety wooden tracks was suspenseful and that the loud noise the cars made as it made its way to the top of the tracks only added to its mystique. Barry always shook his head and laughed, saying that it was just old, tired, and raggedy. In fact, he said that the way it threw us around in its hard metal seats should be a safety hazard. He was convinced he was lucky to have gotten out alive and vowed never to ride it again. I told him that Teshaun and I would be just fine riding it without him. But he did ride it again, over and over throughout the years, at least once every summer until his last.

I closed my eyes and pictured the two of them standing before me, then sniffed the ocean air once more. It was incredible how I felt so close to them whenever I was near the water, even if it wasn't exactly how it used to be. Finally, I walked back to the boardwalk, bought a hotdog and a Sprite from Nathans, then headed back to the train station. Still, I had lived for a moment. I paid my fare and rode the train one stop.

When I arrived at the door, I didn't go into the building right away. Instead, I sat on the stoop and watched the neighborhood boys play football in the street. My memories brought me both pain and comfort. Remembering Teshaun was always tough. I reached into my pocket again; it was there that I found solace. When I had seen enough, I entered the building, creeping through the long hallway, then up the two flights of stairs. I took a deep breath before ringing the bell; I'd thrown away my spare key two years ago.

"Who is it?" the voice behind the door asked.

"It's me," I answered softly.

FIVE

The number 309 at the top of the door stared me in the face. After all these years there was still no peephole, just a heavy metal door and a doorbell. I could hear the footsteps stop at the door. "Who is it?"

"It's me ," I said, shifting my weight from one foot to the other..

Dad's voice barked back. "Me who?"

"Gabby. I mean Gabrielle," I said, louder this time.

Suddenly, the door was unlocked and Daddy pulled me into his arms. "Gabrielle, is it really you?"

"Yes, Dad, it's really me," I confirmed as I loosened myself from his grasp.

"Oh. It's so good to see you. Come in and sit down." His lips were chapped but his smile was sincere.

I came in and took a seat in a blue flowered arm chair. Looking around I could see that not much had changed at home. The oversized Early American styled couches still lined the perimeter of the room while Mom's porcelain knickknacks decorated the oak shelves. The same oak coffee table was set in the middle of the floor. I noticed the scratches and marks my brother and I had put on it as we were growing up. Mom's hanging ferns decorated the foyer. And Dad's wildlife magazine collection were still displayed in an oak magazine rack.

"Where exactly have you been staying? Your mother and I've been worried sick about you," he said.

"Where is Mom?"

"She's still down at the church," Dad waved his hand to indicate his disapproval. "I left her there with the car and walked home."

I looked at the grandfather clock in the corner. "I see."

Dad scratched his forehead as if he was trying to remember the answer to my question.

"They're running the food pantry today after service," Dad said.

I nodded. "That makes sense."

"You know your mother-always taking care of people." Dad's voice was gruff from years of smoking, quitting, then restarting.

"Yep, that' s Mom." I felt awkward sitting in my parent's home after not speaking to them for so many months.

"What about you? How've you been?" He looked me up and down, frowning.

"I'm okay." I stood up and walked over to the oak entertainment center.

There I glanced at the framed pictures that graced its shelves. There they were, pictures of all of us, including my Teshaun and Barry. I looked at the pictures but I didn't touch them at first. They were precious.

Dad followed me. "You never call."

"I don't have a cell phone." I picked up a picture of all of us at a Christmas dinner, stared at it curiously, then set it back down.

"Where are you staying now?" Dad spoke anxiously, the lines in his face standing at attention. The years had not been kind to him.

"I'm still staying at a shelter." It was at that moment that I should've told him about our street festival, the event that was so important to Ms. Baptiste. But I let that moment pass.

"Well, why don't you tell me which one you're staying at so we can come visit and make sure you're all right?"

I didn't answer right away. *Should I just ask him?* Instead, I picked up another picture; it was a picture of my brother and I riding our bicycles in the park. "That won't be necessary. I'm all right."

Dad shook his head. "But who can help you out there all alone?"

"I'm helping myself, Dad." I spoke calmly. "And it's not like that. It's more than just a shelter but a program to help women."

"To help women with what?"

"To help them with whatever, job training, domestic violence, drug or alcohol addiction, unemployment, child support, abuse, depression and any other thing."

"Sounds like a lot of mess to be mixed up in," he said.

There it was, the main reason I never wanted to invite him in the first place. "I guess you could say that but that's what I am right now, Dad -a mess," I answered, walking away from the pictures.

"I know you're hurting, Gabrielle, but-"

"But what? You don't know anything about hurting until you've had the kind of pain I have to live with every day." I swallowed my spit before turning away.

"So this is how you want to live, Gabrielle?" Dad threw up his hands in mock surrender. "In a shelter?"

I looked into his eyes. "Please call me Gabby. Sometimes I'm not sure how I want to live but I'm just grateful that after a year of therapy, I do want to live. Don't you understand that?"

"Oh, don't say that," Dad said, sternly.

"Why not? It's the truth," I squealed.

Dad looked horrified. "You can't mean that."

"I do mean it." Despite my best efforts, my eyes began to fill up with tears. "Why did it

have to be my Barry and Teshaun? Why me?"

"I can't answer that, Baby Doll ," Dad said, softly as he reached out to me.

I backed away. "Then I can't accept what you're telling me. Something broke inside me and I can't be your Baby Doll anymore."

Dad rubbed his hands together the way he always did when he was nervous. "Your mother and I miss you and we're worried about you."

I could see the fear in his eyes. "Don't worry about me. I'm okay."

Dad took two steps towards me. "But it has been two long, hard years and we want you to come home."

I shook my head back and forth. "I don't have a home anymore."

"Yes, of course you do. Our home is your home. Please, Gabrielle," Dad pleaded.

I walked close to him and sniffed his clothes, then spat out, "If you really wanted me home, you'd stop drinking."

Dad opened his mouth wide with surprise. "Here we go again. What has my drinking got to do with anything?"

"Are you kidding me? It has to do with everything." I shook my head. "I lost my whole family, my whole life because of one drunk driver. But my own father doesn't care enough about me, my mother, or himself to stop driving around drunk. The truth is I can't stand the sight of you."

Dad pointed his bony finger at me. "Gabrielle, you watch yourself, young lady."

"You've been drinking ever since I can remember. And it has only gotten worse; what's

going to happen when you have an accident one of these days? By yourself or with mom? Or God forbid-on that bus of yours," I spat out.

"Now you know I never drink before going to work."

"Humph. Either way you could kill someone but you don't even seem to care. Even to respect your own grandson's and son in law's memory; you still drink and drive."

Dad pointed his thick finger at me. "That's not true."

"Oh it's true and you're only lying to yourself." I walked up and sniffed him once again "Is that Johnnie Walker Red I smell under your Old Spice cologne?"

"Gabrielle-"

"I thought so." I waved my hands. "Never mind. It's pointless."

"Gabrielle McBay-," Dad started

I clenched my teeth. "I'd rather you not call me that."

"Why not?"

"Because it just reminds me of who I used to be; I'm not her anymore. Just call me

Gabby. Gabrielle died two years ago on the floor of that hospital room."

Dad took my hands in his. "You're beautiful and smart. You used to be one of the best litigators in the whole country."

"Used to be." I closed my eyes as I remembered. "A lot of things used to be. I used to be happy until I lost my husband and my son. They were my whole world. Don't you understand that?" I loosed my hands from his.

Dad took me by my shoulders and shook me a little. "You've got to snap out of it. It has been two whole years now."

"So what does that mean? Two years? Is two years supposed to erase my memories? Is two years supposed to bring them back? What can two years do for me?"

"Two years was supposed to allow you to heal but you've been fighting the process the whole time," Dad proclaimed. "Pastor Neill has been preaching about-"

"Save it. I don't care about what Pastor Neill has to say. And then you're going to tell me what *he* has to say when you're the biggest hypocrite out there. Oh, I don't think so."

"Gabrielle…"

"And this conversation is over." I walked quickly towards the door. "Tell Mom that I'm sorry I missed her. Maybe next time."

"Wait, you're not going to at least wait for your mother to get home?"

"No, I've got to get back uptown," I huffed.

"But I can drive you anywhere you need to go. Please stay for lunch or dinner." Dad pleaded.

There was so much sadness in his eyes that they were almost a mirror image of mine.

"No thanks," I said.

"I know you're hurting but healing is a process." Dad stepped towards me.

"Process you say. Oh what do you know about healing or process? How many AA meetings have you gone to?" I was filled with anger. "I've been to therapy and it still hurts like it was yesterday."

"I know and I didn't say it wouldn't hurt but you've got to move on. Barry would want you to move on."

"I have moved on," I smirked.

Dad pounded his fist against the side table and the lamp shook. "No, you've given up."

I shrugged my shoulders, although I knew that response would upset him. "What's the difference? Moving on is moving on no matter how I choose to do it."

Dad lifted his head and looked me in the eyes. "Don't say that. Your mother and I love you very much."

"Humph." I shook my head in utter disbelief. "How can you stand there with alcohol on your breath and say that you love me, knowing everything I ever cared about is gone because of alcohol?"

"Gabrielle-"

"No, don't bother. I'm done." And I ran downstairs and out of the building without looking back.

It was raining so I covered my head with my backpack. I felt the cold raindrops as they soaked my clothes. I could hardly see anything because it was raining so hard. Water began to fill my sneakers as I ran across the street, through the intersection. All of a sudden I heard the honk of a car horn as a car swerved, brakes shrieked, drowning out Dad's voice, "Gabrielle."

By the time I opened my eyes, I was on the ground. A big faced man was hovering over me but it wasn't my dad. He had beady eyes and thick eyebrows.

He kneeled down beside me. "Lady, are you all right?"

I propped myself up on my elbows. "Yeah, what happened?"

"I don't know. You came running into the street. I moved out of the way so I wouldn't hit you and I don't know, you must've passed out or something," the man said.

He helped me up as I spotted the open door on his taxi and realized he was the driver.

Just as I stood up, Dad reached the middle of the street where we were standing. "Are you okay?

"I'm okay, I said, dusting off my clothes." It was still drizzling.

Dad looked at the taxi driver with a frown, then at me. "Are you sure?"

"Hey, I'm sorry Sir, but she ran right out in front of my car. I tried to stop," the taxi driver said.

Dad ignored him. "Gabrielle, are you all right, baby?"

My head was spinning. "I'm fine."

Dad looked me up and down in disbelief. "Are you sure you're all right?"

"Yeah, I'm sure. But I've got to get out of here. I've got to get out of this rain." I grabbed my backpack and disappeared down the block and slid into the subway station.

"Gabrielle, wait…" I heard my father's voice calling for me long after I was underground.

SIX

By the time the train arrived back in Manhattan, it was time to go to work. So I climbed up the subway steps and then walked the two blocks to The Old Country Bakery. There I put in exactly fifteen hours a week. It wasn't perfectly part-time since I didn't do at least twenty hours but I was grateful to have something nonetheless. The first year I lived at the shelter I was no good to anyone. I didn't want a job or money. I didn't care about anything. By the second year I began to want things on occasion, little things I couldn't buy. A job was, of course, a way to get those things. Besides, working at the small bakery kept me busy. There were only so many hours I could spend at the library, or in therapy. Having a job gave me something to do even if it was just putting multi-colored sprinkles on cupcakes. I had value.

The Old Country Bakery was known around the neighborhood for making the best peach cobbler in Harlem. It was a family owned business run by the Martins family from Mississippi. The Martins were grooming their oldest son, Lawrence Jr., to take over the business in the coming years so most days I was subject to his mood swings. I usually ran the cash register and did a little baking from time to time. Yet, the truth of the matter was that I was a pretty good cook, something I'd picked up from my own mother, who spent countless hours in the kitchen. Cooking helped to soothe my troubled soul.

I took my place behind the counter and tied on my apron. And once I was settled in, the sweet aroma of peach cobblers, sweet potato pies, banana pudding, red velvet cake, and pound cake wafted from the massive oven.

Before long, my co-worker and the closest thing I had to a friend my own age, Uma, came into the shop. As soon as Uma walked in, I was asked to end my shift. *Cheapskate!* The bakery couldn't stand going a penny over budget. I didn't argue although everything in me wanted to. I just went to the tiny restroom and stripped out of my uniform. When I returned, I greeted Uma with a pat on the shoulder before heading to the door.

Uma was a soft spoken young woman in her mid-thirties. An Indian immigrant, she wore Indian garb and a colorful scarf on her head, covering her long, black silky hair. She'd moved to the United States from New Delhi with her mother after her parents divorced. I met her on the first night I slept on the streets. Seeing how clean and nicely manicured I was, she was concerned about seeing me asleep on a bus stop bench. She stopped to ask if I was okay and if I needed bus fare to get home. When I told her that I no longer had a home, which was only partially true, she bought me a hotdog, a hot pretzel and a can of Sprite from a nearby food vendor. Before I knew it, we became friends. The next day she brought me a blanket, a slice of pizza, and the telephone number of The Home Again Women's Transitional shelter; she and her mother had once stayed there until they got on their feet many years ago. It was right there that I knew I would live, despite the pain.

"I saved something for you." Uma handed me a piece of folded paper.

"What is it?"

When I opened it, I saw job listings.

"I printed them out for you because I know you don't have a computer."

"Thanks Uma. I'll look into them as soon as I get a chance."

"I know your extension is almost up so..." Uma looked at me sheepishly.

"I know. I'll figure something out."

I reached into my pocket and squeezed what gave me comfort.

"I also heard about a program for the homeless at a church-"She handed me a flyer.

"Thanks but no thanks." I dumped it into the trash can, then turned to leave.

Harden not your heart.

"I'm sorry. I didn't mean to upset you," she yelled out. "You know I care about you, Gabby."

Uma looked remorseful but I didn't care. I fanned her away with my hand, and then shook my head, wondering what kind of mixed signals I'd been giving for her to think I would ever be interested in receiving help from a church. Didn't I make it clear enough that I had no more faith? What would make her think anything could change that?

As I went out the front door, I heard Uma's voice still calling me softly, but I never turned back.

"Go home," I was told by the manager. But home was an elusive word for someone who had no real place to go. And I found myself back on the streets watching people go by. With only two more months at the shelter, if I disappeared now, I wouldn't have to endure this nonsense. "Chile, you can't keep running forever," Ms. Baptiste's words reverberated in my head.

I stopped by the library on the way home and stayed huddled in a corner reading until it was time for closing. With so much weighing heavily on my mind, I'd fallen asleep for a few minutes and almost missed the last call. They were about to turn the lights out on me when I crawled out from the back. Luckily, I was able to check out three books before they shut the computers down for the evening. Then I grabbed my things and started walking down 125th street towards home.

Where is home for the homeless? I recalled my three story colonial home , complete with a mother in law suite and a pool house. There was a front yard , complete with a lovely rose garden and a back yard with a stone fire pit, a pavilion, and a deck built onto our family room. In the summertime, we spent our time swimming in our pool, and had barbecues with our neighbors in our back yard. Often we would just walk along the coast, enjoying the ocean spray.

Barry was the more outgoing one, the life of the party since college but I was the one who held it all together. Teshaun followed in his father's footsteps with several groups of friends, ranging from his teammates, classmates, and neighborhood kids always stopping by the house at all times of day and night. The house had my trendsetting stamp on it, filled with velvet curtains and matching backdrops, contemporary handcrafted crystal and marble pieces from Boca do Lobo nestled amongst plush Fendi de Casa curved seating. I'd put my unique touch on everything I put my hands on, including the Carrocel stone tops and hand polished lacquer in the kitchen. I'd adored that house until the month I gave it all up. *And without hesitation, I'd do it all over again.*

Back at the shelter that evening I slipped by the security guard, Mr. Williams, who was fast asleep at the front door, and quietly snuck into our common area. Ms. Baptiste was sitting on one of the vinyl couches reading the New York Times and drinking coffee.

Ms. Baptiste looked over her reading glasses. "How was your day?"

I walked around the back of the couch. "Lawrence sent me home early so I didn't get my hours and I can't seem to stop thinking about the past today."

Ms. Baptiste put her newspaper down and took a sip of her tea. "Well, you could've gone to church with me today." Ms. Baptiste swatted me, playfully.

I frowned up my whole face. "No, thanks."

"It's your life, dear." She continued to read her newspaper. "But tomorrow isn't promised to us…"

"No one knows that better than me." I wouldn't give her the satisfaction of eye contact. I didn't want her to know what an influence she had on me. "I did finally go home though, "I continued.

"Good for you. And how did that turn out?" She twisted her lips.

I sat down next to her. "I saw my dad."

"And your mom?"

I shook my head. "She wasn't home from church yet."

"And you didn't wait for her?"

I grunted first. "I didn't feel like being bothered with the hypocrisy."

"Excuse me…"

"I went to let them know that I'm all right so they won't worry but when I saw my dad it was the same old thing-alcohol on his breath. It makes me sick to my stomach. It makes me think of Barry and Teshaun and how a drunk driver killed them both, without even thinking."

Ms. Baptiste shook her head. "But your father didn't kill them, Gabby."

"I know that but he might as well have. He drives around town intoxicated all the time and my mom sees it but doesn't see it. Once he actually crashed one of our cars, ran into a light post on the corner. I'm sure he was drunk but he never reported it to his insurance. And it's like she doesn't smell it on his breath or see the sway in his step, or hear the violence on his lips." I could feel my anger rising in me.

Ms. Baptiste pursed her lips. "Alcoholism is a serious disease."

I sucked my teeth. "Tell that to my mom."

Ms. Baptiste looked up at me. "What do you want her to do?"

"I want her to admit that he's an alcoholic, that he needs help so he can stop being a menace to public safety. She can help everybody else with their problems, everyone except her own husband." I was losing control.

"Have you ever told her that?"

"Yes, many times." I clenched my fists together. "But after a while I just got fed up. He guzzles down beers throughout the day, then brandy after dinner. Not to mention what he carries in his thermos to work…it's not soup."

"Does she drink with him?"

I sucked my teeth. "Nope. She's a one hundred percent java drinker. Nothing but hot black coffee passes her lips. I mean the most I'd ever seen her drink was a glass of champagne at my brother's wedding and she had to be coaxed into doing that."

Ms. Baptiste twirled one of her locs with her finger. "Then why do you think she doesn't recognize that there's a problem?"

I hopped off of the couch. "That's what I don't understand. It's so obvious."

"Maybe it's not obvious to her, for whatever reason. Just keep praying for her, Gabby."

"You know I don't pray anymore." I wasn't going to argue with Ms. Baptiste.

"Well, you should." Ms. Baptiste took a deep breath. "I'm sure your mother would've liked to see you, hear from you."

"I'll call her in a couple of days," I said.

Ms. Baptiste took off her glasses and placed them in her lap. "It seems to me that you're trying to make her suffer."

"No, I just can't take looking at the two of them. I lost my whole world because somebody decided to drink and drive. And guess what? That driver is alive, incarcerated but alive. My family is dead…dead." I caught the tears before they fell down my face.

"I'm sorry, Gabby. I don't have all the answers." Ms. Baptiste paused. "Sweetie, you've got to leave it all in God's hands. He is faithful to work everything out. I can promise you that," Ms. Baptiste said.

I came right up to her face. "I don't believe in those promises anymore."

"I know you don't but I'm believing enough for the both of us." Without warning, Ms. Baptiste wrapped her thick arms around me.

It reminded me of my mother's hugs and I let myself get lost in its warmth for a moment, then peeled myself away. "Thanks."

"Don't you want any dinner?"

"Not really." I began climbing the stairs to my room, without looking back at her. "I had a hot pretzel earlier."

"A nice gentleman from the neighborhood called and offered to volunteer some of his time to help us prepare for the event," Ms. Baptiste hollered after me.

"Good," I said. The more volunteers she had, the less work the rest of us had to do. The truth was I hadn't really prepared for any event since *the funeral* two years ago.

Maybe Ms. Baptiste had a point; maybe I was letting life pass me by. I'd stopped attending the group therapy sessions a few months ago, stopped working on myself altogether. I got tired of sitting through the long, sad rantings of every woman in the shelter without ever sharing a word about myself. It seemed both unfair and counterproductive so I stopped going. Ms. Baptiste threatened to put me out the first week I didn't show up but by the fifth time, she realized that I wasn't going to participate no matter what. Eventually, she arranged for me to have private therapy sessions twice a month through a connection of hers. I'm sure that certainly eased her conscience. As expected, nothing took away the pain; I was still broken in places no one could see. But I guess therapy taught me pain management.

When I got to my room, Ashley was sitting on the floor putting rollers into her hair.

Ashley spun around to face me. "I was wondering where you've been."

"Nowhere really. Just dropped by my parent's house earlier today."

"Your parents' house? That sounds kind of big, huh?"

"Not really. My dad's still drinking and my mom is still helping him drink so…"

Ashley put her last roller into her long blonde hair. "Sorry to hear that. If it makes you feel any better my parents won't even speak to me."

I took out my new books from my backpack but didn't respond.

"You sure do love to read. You must've been a good student when you were in school huh."

"I guess you could say that," I answered, honestly.

Ashley stood to her feet. "Tomorrow we start getting ready for the street party festival thingy. That's all Ms. Baptiste has been talking about all day."

I grinned. "Yep and I invited two people."

Ashley opened her eyes and mouth wide. "Wow, you've never invited anybody to anything before."

"Well, I did today-I met a kid named Caleb and he'll have to bring his mom or dad I guess. He bought two tickets." I grinned again.

Ashley grabbed me by the arm as I passed by. "What got into you?"

I gently pulled away from her. "He kind of saw the raffle tickets when I dropped them and he asked to come."

"So he invited himself?"

"Kind of… He wants to win a PlayStation prize and…he reminds me of someone."

"How did you find this kid anyway?"

"I didn't find him; I guess he found me at the library. He was there with some troublemaking kids at first but he turned out to be okay-"

"Good for you Ashley giggled. "I'd better get on my game and invite some people too."

"Yeah, you'd better do that. Ms. Baptiste is expecting a good turn out." I went into the bathroom and shut the door.

Ashley banged on the door. "No, really- what's got into you, girl?"

"I don't know." I couldn't help but smile but underneath it all, I knew this would be my last event at the shelter.

SEVEN

DEVIN

Devin only stopped by his apartment after work to change into a pair of old jeans and a t-shirt. He had promised to stop by The Home Again Shelter today and he didn't want to be late. He was just about to grab a quick snack when he heard the doorbell ring. He wondered who it was. Not surprisingly, it was his old friend Simon. They had been friends since college and they usually hung out together at least once or twice a month. On a good day, they would go shoot some hoops, or work out together at the gym. But today he didn't have time for any of that.

Devin opened the door slowly.

Simon came in and took a seat in a leather arm chair. "Hey bruh, what's up?"

"Nothing, man." Devin sat on the couch. "What's up with you?"

Simon let out a little yawn. "Just working, dude-tired."

"Hey, at least you're holding it down and making it happen," Devin said.

Simon answered, "I don't know about all of that, bruh but it's a job."

"It's just a job to you? You kidding me? I'd love to have the opportunity to teach at a college." Devin took off his glasses and placed them on the folding table.

"Don't be too sure." Simon flipped through a sports magazine that was in the chair beside him. Simon put the magazine down. "Believe me, you can have it."

"You sound like you don't like it anymore?"

"I used to for the first couple of years but being an adjunct professor is not as good as it may sound."

"Okay."

"Don't get me wrong. With two of them being virtual, I'm working three colleges at the same time so the money is rolling in but I'm burned out all the time. I'm always looking at a computer screen and with my in person job I'm always running late."

Devin chuckled. "Same Simon."

Now I'm ready to move on; I'm ready to do something else, you know?"

Devin continued over to the kitchen counter. "I hear that. I was about to make myself a sandwich. You want one?"

"Nah. I already ate," Simon said.

Devin opened his eyes wide. "You're turning down food?"

"What you trying to say?"

"Nothing at all." Devin held up both hands in mock surrender. "Anyway, I get it man. I'm kind of burned out too."

"You, Mr. Mentor of the year?"

"I really like working with the kids but now that I've finished up my doctorate, I'm ready to put all of this knowledge to greater use."

"Dr. Devin Ramos," Simon said in an extra deep voice. "What do you want to do exactly?"

"Maybe I want to work inside a big office helping to make some big decisions, the kind that affect all these kids, not just the ones in my classroom." Devin placed a few pieces of meat onto a piece of rye bread, then added cheese, chopped a few peppers and put them onto his sandwich along with mayonnaise and mustard.

"You've got some lofty dreams, man." Simon looked up to the ceiling.

"I just want to make a real difference." Devin bit into his sandwich. "You want a drink, man?"

"Sure. What you got?"

Devin threw bottled water to Simon.

Simon caught it. "Thanks, man. You already make a difference , working with those hard headed kids but I hear you, bruh."

Devin knew that he was seldom able to get into Simon's head. Perhaps now was a good opportunity. "What about you? What do you want?"

"I want to leave academia and maybe go back to corporate America. Maybe get into tech; that's where the real money is at." Simon opened his water and guzzled it.

"Is that all you're looking for-money?"

Simon began to laugh out loud. "Look, I don't have everything figured out but when I do I'll let you know. All right?"

"No doubt." Devin continued, "You know what I want more than anything right now though?"

"Nah, not a clue. What?"

"A good woman."

Simon started grinning and rubbing his hands together. "But dude there are plenty of women out here."

Devin shook his head and waved his hands. "But that's not what I'm talking about, man.

I want more."

Simon looked over his glasses at him. "More what?"

"I know this is going to sound corny but more of a meaningful relationship."

Simon fell backwards with laughter. "Okay, where is the real Devin?"

"Naw, man; I'm serious. It gets lonely sometimes, even when I'm dating. Sometimes it feels so fake. pointless."

"Fake? That's new." Simon chuckled.

"No, it's not new." Devin looked serious. "I've been feeling this way for a while now."

"Really? That's probably just old age talking."

"Maybe," Devin answered, solemnly.

"Just kidding. You're not old. You're serious, huh?" Simon shook his head. "Never knew you felt that way, man. I mean that's deep and all but you're by yourself on that; I'm definitely not ready to settle down again. Not after my killer divorce; I'm still trying to recover."

"I know but I am. I haven't even gotten to the altar once," Devin said.

"Consider yourself lucky,"

Devin punched Simon in the arm. "You're out of order…"

"I'm just saying…"

"I don't need any warnings. What I need is to meet the right woman."

"The *right* woman? Well, good luck with that. I'm happy these days when I meet *any* woman."

"Maybe that's your problem." Devin lifted his hands into the air. "Raise your standards a little."

Simon leaned back in his chair. "Hey, I thought we were talking about your problem-not mine."

"True." Devin put out his fist and Simon bumped it with his.

"And just where do you intend to meet this *right* woman?"

"I don't know yet, but I've been praying for God to send her to me, or to show me where can find her.

Simon sat up straight. "Whoa. Okay, that's a little too deep for me. But whenever you meet that special woman do me a little favor."

"What's that?"

"Ask her if she has a sister." Simon started to crack up with laughter again.

Devin chuckled. "You're impossible."

Simon looked around the room. "What are you doing this evening anyway?"

"Actually, I volunteered for me and Caleb to help out at a homeless shelter. They're setting up for a street festival."

Simon shook his head. "Street festival? Homeless shelter? You really are desperate, aren't you?"

"What's wrong with helping? Besides, it'll teach Caleb a good lesson."

Simon stood up, fumbling around in his pockets. "Who in the world is Caleb?"

Devin watched him carefully. "One of the science students I've been mentoring."

"Of course." Simon took out a cigarette.

Devin walked to the door and opened it. "Nah, bruh. Take that mess outside."

"Boy, you used to love the smell of smoke." Simon took out his lighter.

"I used to love a lot of things but that was a long time ago. I'm not that guy anymore.." Devin grabbed the lighter from him and held it until Simon stepped outside, then handed it back to him. "You need to quit too."

"Okay, okay, I get it, church boy," Simon huffed, placing both items into his pocket.

Devin stood in the doorway, shaking his head. "You need a lot of help."

"Well, pray for me then." Simon started down the stairs. "Got to go. See ya later, buddy."

"Later," Devin answered before closing the door and bounding down the stairs. "I'm right behind you."

When Devin first arrived at the address with its numbers etched in granite, the first thing he noticed was that it was a brownstone building.

The second thing he noticed was that Home Again was a women's shelter; he was utterly embarrassed. He'd naively assumed that it was a coed homeless shelter, not one only for women. He should have asked Caleb what kind of shelter it was. He stood outside staring at the sign for a few minutes before a lady with long thick locks came to the front door.

A tall, older lady peeked out. "I'm Ms. Baptiste, the director. How may I help you?"

"I was told that you all needed help with some kind of festival," Devin explained.

"Yes, yes, come in, Mr. Ramos." Ms. Baptiste stepped aside so he could enter into the lobby, then led him past a security guard, to the family room. It was very spacious and somewhat old fashioned in design. There was an old wooden upright piano in the corner and Devin wondered which one of them played. "We do need all the help we can get. We don't often get the help of handsome young men like you. Usually just tore up old women like me." She laughed.

Devin kept a straight face. "Ma'am, you are certainly not old enough to joke like that."

"Well you're very kind," she said.

"A student of mine is meeting me here also. His name is Caleb."

"So you're that teacher huh? We need more dedicated teachers in this world."

"Yes, ma'am," Devin answered, wondering exactly what he had gotten himself into.

Ms. Baptiste looked him up and down as if she was studying him. "Serving others is a good lesson to show to a young boy."

Devin rubbed his big hands together as if he was up to something. "That's what I was hoping for."

"You're a good man, Mr. Ramos." Ms. Baptiste patted him on the back. "We need more men like you out here on the battlefield."

Devin was flattered but that wasn't why he did what he did. "I don't know about all that. I'm just trying to do my part, that's all."

"I'm sure it's greatly appreciated by all. Do you have any children of your own?"

Devin eyes turned downward. "No, ma'am."

"That's nothing to be ashamed of, son. I don't have any biological children either. But all of these women here are like my children. Some of them even treat me like I'm their mother."

"That's nice." Devin could see why; he felt totally comfortable here.

"No, it's more than nice; it's my calling," Ms. Baptiste explained quietly. "I'll show you to the kitchen where there are some boxes that need moving and unpacking, chairs that need to be brought up from the basement and things like that."

Just then Devin looked out of the huge bay window and spotted Caleb walking up to the front door. "There he is, my student."

"I'll let him in." Ms. Baptiste opened the front door. "Welcome to Home Again, young man."

"Thanks." Caleb looked nervous.

"Come on in. Your teacher is already here. Sit down and make yourself at home while I go and get the storeroom key." Ms. Baptiste left the room.

"I'm glad you could make it, dude," Devin said.

Caleb whispered, "Not really sure what I'm doing here, though. A party is one thing but hanging out at a shelter is another. I don't know."

"It's good to help. Did you know that many Americans are only a couple of paychecks away from being homeless themselves?"

Caleb shrugged his shoulders. "I never thought about it like that."

"I know you didn't. Neither did I when I was your age. But now that I'm older and I know some things, I help to feed the hungry every Thanksgiving and Christmas. And I like to donate every now and then."

Caleb looked all around him. "That's a good idea I guess."

"Many of the homeless faces you see are just everyday people who fell on hard times and need a hand up, not a hand out, to get back on their feet," Devin explained.

Caleb leaned in. "A lot of 'em seem pretty crazy to me."

"Shhh. You don't want to offend anybody." Devin whispered. "That's because a lot of them have mental illness and there is no place else for them to go. The hospitals won't keep them without insurance or money. Sadly, most of them stay out on the streets because they're afraid of being institutionalized, even by their families."

"Whoa." Caleb asked, "How did you learn all of that?"

"One of my masters degrees is in sociology."

Caleb stared at Devin for a few seconds. "How long were you in school for?"

Devin chuckled. "Too long."

When they looked up, Gabby was coming down the stairs with Ms. Baptiste.

"Hello, Ms. Gabby?" Caleb said.

"Hi, Caleb," Gabby answered. "What are you doing here?"

Ms. Baptiste looked back and forth between Gabby and the guests. "Gabby, you know these two gentlemen."

Gabby stepped forward and waved. "Yes, we've met."

Devin stood up, with his hands in his pockets. "Hello again, Ms. Gabby."

"Hi," Gabby said.

Ms. Baptiste smiled at Gabby. "Well, it's good that you've all met. These two have come to volunteer their time and I never turn down help."

"No, it's good that they're here to help." Gabby smiled. "We don't usually get a lot of help around here."

"So I've heard." Devin looked at Ms. Baptiste and smiled.

Ms. Baptiste grabbed Devin and Caleb by the arms and led them down to the basement. "Well enough small talk; let's get busy."

After toiling downstairs, they finally came up, carrying loads of boxes in their arms. Devin and Caleb fell back onto one of the couches in exhaustion. They each searched the family room for Gabby but she was nowhere to be found.

"Where is that Gabby? I'll bet she's in the kitchen," Ms. Baptiste said. "Gabby."

"Yes ma'am? I'm here." Gabby popped her head in. Sure enough she was wearing an apron, a hairnet and oven mitts.

"Believe it or not Gabby is one of our best cooks here," Ms. Baptiste said, proudly. "Works part-time at The Old Country Bakery up on 127th street too."

Devin could hardly believe his ears. "Does she? "He didn't know anything about cooking but he certainly liked to eat, especially sweets. So the strange little woman was a wonder in the kitchen. Interesting.

For two hours Devin and Caleb carried boxes back and forth, taking short lemonade and ice tea breaks in between multiple trips to the basement. Finally, Gabby sat down next to Caleb. "How did your speech go, young man?"

"It went great." Caleb sat up in his chair.

Gabby put her hand on the side of her face. "Really?"

"Yep, I really did it." Caleb said.

Gabby liked this boy. Clearly, he reminded her of Teshaun. "Okay, good. So what's next for you?"

Caleb shrugged his shoulders. "What do you mean?"

Gabby continued, "So you said a speech at the senator's affair but what will you do for an encore?"

Caleb twiddled his thumbs. "Oh, don't know about that."

"You should start thinking about it." Gabby pointed her finger in his face. "Never let the public forget you; always have a follow up plan."

Caleb looked serious. "You make it sound so important."

"It is important. Your future is important. So work hard and decide what your next step will be. You've got to keep going higher and higher." Gabby wasn't sure what was driving her.

Caleb looked into Gabby's eyes. "What if I don't know how to do that?"

Gabby pointed toward Devin. "I'm sure that people will help you along the way."

Caleb asked, "People like Mr. Ramos?"

"I guess." Gabby shrugged.

Just then, Ms. Baptiste walked back into the room. "Gabby, would you help Mr. Ramos and Caleb. Mr. Ramos to get these things organized? Mr. Ramos, Please follow Gabby." Devin was obviously caught off guard. "Um, sure. No problem."

"Gabby?" Ms. Baptiste asked.

"I don't know what I could possibly be a help with but sure, follow me." Gabby stood up and led the way. She remained quiet and short with her words the entire time but Devin wasn't fooled. He could tell that there was more to this woman than she wanted him to see.

EIGHT

The next day after I'd done my hours at the bakery, I walked home, smelling of fresh buttermilk corn bread. As I walked, I could feel a rushing spring breeze in the air. I pushed my hands deep into my pockets as my fingertips were cold; maybe I was anemic. Once I reached the building, and started to climb the front steps, I found that annoying man from the library at the shelter again. Now a little volunteering never hurt anybody but two days in a row was a bit much. He had an armful of boxes and he was leaning over to stack them onto a pile in the hallway. He seemed to have such a momentum, working up a sweat, that I watched him for a moment.

Finally, I approached him. "What in the world are you doing here again?"

Devin wiped his forehead with a napkin. "Good to see you again too, Ms. Gabby.?" he said in a sarcastic tone.

I put my hands on my hips to hear his idea of an explanation, thinking to myself, *This had better be good.* "What are you doing?"

He chuckled. "Actually, we had an administrative day at the high school today so I was able to leave early. Ms. Baptiste is such a nice lady and this is such a special program she has here that I figured that I'd come by once more to give you all a hand before the event."

"Really?"

"Yep."

"Wait a minute, how do you know about Ms. Baptiste's programs?"

"Well, first of all, I didn't know her at all 'till yesterday. She told me she gives people a place to stay, food to eat, and most importantly, she gives people hope." Devin looked at me sideways. "But to answer your question, Caleb told me about this place. He said he needed a chaperone for the festival because his mom has to work. So here I am. I hope you don't have a problem with me helping out."

"No, why would I?" I scoffed. "Besides, it's not my decision anyway. I've got nothing to do with it."

Devin continued, "But in a way, since they were your tickets, I kind of feel responsible to…"

I held up my hands in front of me. "Look, you don't owe me anything."

"I didn't mean it like that. I-"

Marisol walked into the living room, modeling her tight knit sweater. "Oh, Devin are you still here?"

"I'm still here, getting a little work done." Devin showed his perfectly white teeth. "I don't have my sidekick with me today so I'm moving a little slower."

"Oh, that's okay. You're moving just fine, Papi." Marisol grinned.

Marisol stood there, glaring at Devin as he continued to move the boxes. True enough the muscles in his arms were bulging but that was no excuse for her shameless flirting.

"Marisol, get a hold of yourself," I said with disdain.

"You're right. I've got so many chores, girl." Marisol swayed her big hips until she was out of sight.

Devin laughed.

I didn't blink. "What's so funny?"

"Nothing. She's just very uh…friendly," Devin said.

I crossed my arms in indignation. "I'll bet."

Devin stopped working and stood up straight. "Is there anything wrong with that?"

I never unfolded my arms. "I thought you had serious work to do here, Mr. Ramos."

Devin continued to chuckle. "Please, call me Devin."

"Mr. Devin, I just don't think that we have time to play games."

Devin wiped the sweat from his brow. "You're right."

"Well, if you'd just finish moving this last box here, I'm sure that Mrs. Baptiste would be grateful." I tried not to sound condescending.

Finally, Devin pushed the boxes neatly into a corner. "Don't worry, I'm done now so…"

"Good." I flashed a fake smile.

"I like your uniform." Devin pointed to the white stripe on my shirt. "Old Country Bakery is it?"

I looked down at my outfit. "Oh, this old thing. I usually change before I leave work."

Ms. Baptiste came downstairs. "Thank you, Devin, dear. Are you done?"

Devin headed toward the door. "I am, Ms. Baptiste. I'm gonna get going now cause I've got mountains of quizzes to grade at home so…"

"I'm sure you do. Thanks so much for lending us your muscles just for a little while. Tell

Caleb that we missed him." Ms. Baptiste escorted him to the exit.

Devin smiled softly. "I will. I would've brought him but you know kids…"

"I do. I'm sure this is the last place he's trying to spend all his free time." Ms. Baptiste laughed. "Take care now."

Devin stopped in front of the door, shook Mr. William's hand, and looked back at us. "You too and I'll see ya around, Gabby."

"See ya," I said.

"Ms. Baptiste closed the door behind Devin. "That Devin seems to be quite a gentleman."

She walked to the living room with me right on her heels. Marisol was already dusting the furniture in the living room.

"He's all right. Nothing special." I turned up my lips.

Ms. Baptiste pushed her glasses up on her nose. "What's not special about him? This was his second day coming and he's helped us out here a whole lot."

"He's okay, I guess," I said.

"He looks pretty good to me, chica."Marisol twirled the dust cloth around in her hand.

Ms. Baptiste and I both gave Marisol a look.

"That's your problem, Marisol hot pants."Ms. Baptiste didn't crack a smile. "And stop flinging that dust around everywhere."

"Ooh that hurt." Marisol put her hand on her heart.

Ms. Baptiste turned her attention back to me. "So what is it that you don't like about him?"

I plopped down on the couch. "I don't know exactly; I just don't trust him."

Ms. Baptiste continued. "Has he given you any reason to suspect him of anything shady?"

"Not exactly," I said.

"So that's all you-Gabby being skeptical again."

"Loco Gabby," Marisol said.

I pushed Marisol, playfully. "I've got to be."

Ms. Baptiste shook her head. "To protect yourself, right?"

I looked straight at Ms. Baptiste. "I know you're mocking me, but yes. He's always so, so…"

Marisol waved her hands. "Good looking?"

I looked at Marisol. "Would you please stop. Don't you already have a boyfriend?"

"Sorry." Marisol giggled before leaving the room.

"Cheerful. That's what he is," Ms. Baptiste said.

Gabby smirked, "Yeah and nobody is like that all the time."

"Of course not because he's human." Ms. Baptiste shook her head. "But that still doesn't mean he's not a nice person."

"But we're always getting into it." I stood up to face Ms. Baptiste. "He's very opinionated."

Ms. Baptiste put her hands on her hips. "Like you are."

"Maybe." I hated to acknowledge it but she was right.

"I've never had a problem with him," Ms. Baptiste said.

"That's because he was too busy giving me a hard time. He reminds me of an old boss I once had, who was a slave driver." I balled up my fists and growled. "Thinks he knows every single thing."

Ms. Baptiste looked at me funny. "I see that he did upset you, huh?" Ms. Baptiste left the living room and went to her office

I followed close behind her. "He's just a lot to deal with. I never knew that selling Caleb tickets to the festival was going to turn out like this but I'll be glad when it's over."

"I'll bet you will." Ms. Baptiste chuckled and I got the feeling that she wasn't taking me seriously.

"By the way, may I use the phone? I want to try inviting my parents one last time."

"No problem." Ms. Baptiste walked out of her office.

I dialed the number and listened to it ring three times before I heard my mother's voice.

"Hi, Mom," I said.

I could hear her surprise. "Gabby, is that you?

"Yeah, Mom, it's me."

"So good to hear your voice," Mom said.

"Same here." I needed to make it quick. "Look, at the place where I'm staying, we're having a street festival next week. It's a fundraiser and we invite all kinds of people to support us."

Mom paused. "Sounds interesting."

I took a deep breath, then spat it out. "Do you think you and Dad might like to come?"

I waited to hear the rejection but instead Mom started to cry on the phone. "Anything to be able to see you, Gabby, and to know that you're all right."

"Okay, it's okay Mom. The name of the shelter is Home Again Women's Transitional Shelter and we're on the corner of 125th and Front Street. It's actually on next Wednesday. Don't ask me why."

"We'll be there." But Mom's voice went cold.

I probed, "Are you sure?"

Mom snapped, "I said we'll be there, didn't I?"

"Okay, okay. I'll see you next week." I'd done it and for better or for worse, I felt relieved.

"See you then, Gabby," Mom said before hanging up the phone.

What was all of that about?

Ms. Baptiste walked back into the room. "I hope you don't mind but I invited that nice young man and Caleb over for dinner later this evening. I figured it would give me a chance to thank them for all of their hard work."

I used my high pitched voice. "Couldn't we just send them a thank you card?"

Ms. Baptiste frowned. "No, that's so impersonal. I couldn't do that. Besides, we've got lots of food. Better belly buss dan good food waste."

An instant headache came on. "Please not tonight. I'm not in the mood to entertain."

"Gabrielle McBay, you stop being hateful like that. Now that boy was as thin as a rail when I met him and he said his mother always works double shifts. And that teacher is single so you know he's not getting any home cooked meals on a consistent basis." Ms. Baptiste clapped her hands. "And I want to serve them some homemade curried crab and dumplings, macaroni pie, ox- tails and rice. So get with the program, gal."

"Yes Ma'am," I said.

Ms. Baptistelooked over towards the kitchen. "We'll make them a good supper, and then we'll give them some to go trays to last them for the rest of the week. Everyone is not as fortunate as we are to eat as well as we do."

"I know." I knew that she was right and that I should feel ashamed but the truth was that I didn't.

"Now I can't help it if you don't feel like being social. When the spirit tells me to show someone love, I have to be obedient." Ms. Baptiste walked away with what she called her island strut.

And I was left carrying the bag of burdens.

When Devin and Caleb arrived that evening, I was in the kitchen preparing a culinary masterpiece. Marisol and Ernestine were helping me with the meal while Ashley and Shelira were fixing up the dining room.

I heard the women laughing heartily in the next room and knew that the guests were here.

"Gabby, let's go." I heard Ms. Baptiste say.

"Here I am." I came out with the serving cart loaded with the curried crab and dumplings, macaroni pie, oxtails, and rice."

"What a spread," Devin said. "Thank you all for having us."

"Yeah, uh. Thanks." Caleb looked uncomfortable sitting amongst so many women and children.

The women mumbled amongst themselves, probably wondering what these two men were doing there again. The children ignored the guests and acted like they usually did, talking and playing as they ate.

"Caleb is a little shy but we're both very grateful to be here. May God bless all of you," Devin said.

I rolled my eyes at his phoniness. *What a player.* I figured that he was enjoying being the center of attention, especially with all of these women.

Ernestine, Marisol and I, wearing our aprons and hairnets, served the food to everyone.

Then we sat down to eat. Ms. Baptiste blessed the food and everyone broke bread together. Devin kept to himself and didn't really join in on the many individual conversations that were going on around him.

Finally, he asked, "So, Ms. Baptiste how long have you been having this street festival?"

Ms. Baptiste smiled. "We've been doing it for the past ten years. Why?"

Devin put a forkful of food into his mouth. "Because I think it's such a good way to connect with the community."

I rolled my eyes again. He was so full of it I wondered if he was running for public office.

"It's my way of giving back and it has become my life's work. I don't know what I'd do without these ladies." Ms. Baptiste looked all around her and smiled.

The women said, "Aww, we love you too, Ms. Baptiste," mostly in unison. Some of them stood up and hugged her. Others just smiled from across the tables. I sat back with my arms crossed, sucking my teeth and waiting for this show to be over.

When I was in the kitchen washing the dishes, Devin came over to me. "I know that you probably planned this whole meal and it was delicious so a special thanks to you."

I was startled. "You're welcome. But I-"

"This is what community is all about." Devin winked at me and left the kitchen.

He was smooth. I'd give him that. So I felt bad for not wanting him to be there but he was always saying or doing something that irritated me. I couldn't put my finger on it but it was there.

I dried my hands and took off my apron. Then I tiptoed into the dining room where Caleb was telling Ms. Baptiste about school. I listened to him from the background and was impressed with how intelligent he sounded. He so reminded me of my Teshaun, I reached into my pocket and squeezed. It hurt my heart to think of my son not being here to enjoy the activities that Caleb discussed. He told Ms. Baptiste that he liked basketball and football, even soccer, and science, which was his first love.

"I want to be a biophysicist," he told Ms. Baptiste.

"Ooh, I can't even pronounce that one." Ms. Baptiste swung her silver laced locks around. "Good luck to you, son. You do your thing and don't let anything stand in your way."

Caleb looked directly at Ms. Baptiste. "I won't. My mom works very hard so that I can have everything I need. She's always telling me to stay out of the streets, to keep my record clean, and my GPA high so I can get a scholarship to a good college. And I won't let anything mess that up."

"Good for you, Caleb. "I didn't mean to join the conversation but there was something about his words that inspired me. "Your mother is right."

Everyone turned to look at me. Most of the women had dispersed to their rooms and only a few children remained, sitting at tables, making a mess. *What are they looking at? Haven't they ever heard someone with an opinion before?*

I walked through the aisles gathering the plates and bringing them to the kitchen.

"Let me help you with that," Devin said, taking many of the dishes from me.

"Thanks." I followed behind him. His massive frame overshadowed mine.

Devin leaned against the wall. "I guess I'll see you at the festival."

"Sure; I'll see you then." I continued to clean up.

Ms. Baptiste came in with Caleb on her heels. "Oh there you are, Devin dear. Thanks again for coming. It has been a joy having both of you but I think this young man may be ready to go."

Caleb began to smile. "It's just that I've got to make an important phone call."

"I can imagine. To a girl, I'm sure." Devin gave him a playful punch.

Caleb swooned. "Not just any girl, the senator's daughter."

Devin said his goodbyes and walked out with Caleb but I noticed that Devin no longer looked happy.

CHAPTER
NINE

It was finally the day of The Home Again's Street Festival. We had worked and waited for two weeks and now it was finally here. The sun shone bright and promising in the sky. *No rain today.* I put on my best outfit which was a pink sun dress that a local charity group had given me a few months ago. I'd never worn it because it didn't seem to fit my mood. But today was different. We were trying to raise enough money to make a difference in the lives of these women. It wasn't about me. Yet, since I'd personally invited my parents, I needed everything to go smoothly. *Pull it together. Everything in its place.*

I wanted to look pretty. I brushed my hair and fluffed it out so that my naturally curly hair had enough volume. I stared at myself in the mirror, examining my skin. The sun had brought a little more color to my cheeks lately.

"Hey, what's up?" Ashley said as she popped into the room. "Ooh, don't you look nice."

"Thanks. If only I could add a little color to my lips."

"What about those Avon packets that charity group dropped off to us a couple of months ago."

I must've been looking at her like I didn't know what in the world she was talking about.

Ashley put two fingers together to indicate length. "You know the sample packets?"

"Oh yeah, the samples. They must be around here somewhere." I started looking on top of my chest of drawers. There was nothing.

Ashley sucked her teeth. "They must be somewhere cause I know you never used them."

I stopped and gave her a look. "And how do you know so much about my life?"

Ashley didn't hesitate. "Cause I look at you every day and you never fix yourself up."

I looked through my drawers until I finally found them. "Here they are." I pulled two lip gloss samples from the bag. First I tried the rosy colored one on my cheek.

"Nope too bright for you." Ashley shook her head.

"Okay let's try the next one." I placed the mauve colored one against my other cheek

Ashley snapped her fingers. "Bingo."

I turned to show both cheeks. "Really?"

"Yeah; it's perfect on you." Ashley nodded, turning my face from side to side "Okay so here goes." So I used tissue to wipe the two trial smears off of my cheeks, took up the lip gloss , puckered up, and on it went. Instantly, I was pleased with my appearance.

"You look good, girl." Ashley clapped.

I twirled in the mirror. "Thanks. I could use some wedge heeled sandals, though."

"That's okay. Sneakers always work, especially on these streets." Ashley snapped her fingers.

"I guess you're right." I looked down at my feet. "I think a little lotion is in order too. I can't face the public ashy."

"No, you can't." Ashley and I both laughed.

I pulled out a sample lotion and put some onto my legs and feet. My hands and arms were already fine for whatever reason. Then I slipped into my canvas shoes.

"Now this public you're concerned about wouldn't have anything to do with that guy huh?"

"What guy?"

Ashley grinned. "You know the one who has been hanging out around here lately, helping out and everything."

"Are you insane? Why would I care about him?"

"I don't know. Just checking, that's all." Ashley fanned me away. "I forgot for a minute that you're not like the rest of us. I forgot you don't want happiness."

"Humph." I shot her a look. "I just don't believe in certain things anymore. That doesn't mean I can't look good for the festival."

"Whatever." Ashley shook her head.

All that mattered was that for this particular occasion, I was at least cute; that was the most that I could ask for.

At Ms. Baptiste's insistence, I'd finally gotten around to inviting my parents to the festival so I looked forward to seeing Mom this time. *I just hoped Dad would be sober.* I knew they probably wouldn't stay very long because they weren't the most social couple but at least I would have met my personal quota for inviting people.

I looked over at Ashley who was busy squeezing into a pair of skin tight jeans; they were ripped and faded but that was her style. She pulled an old yellow cropped shirt over her head, careful not to mess up her hairdo. Her long silky hair was done in cornbraids; Ernestine had done it for her.

I smiled at her. "Are you ready to go downstairs?"

"Yeah, sure, but you go on down first while I straighten out this bed. You know how Ms. Baptiste is."

It sounded like an excuse to me. "Okay, I'll meet you downstairs." I closed the door to the room, wondering what Ashley would be doing when I left. She'd been acting very moody lately, secretive even. Those were two of the signs that she was *using* again. *I hoped I was wrong about her.*

"I'll be right down," I could hear her say as I walked away.

When I reached the bottom of the stairs I was greeted by all of the hustle and bustle of the upcoming event.

"Gabby, finally! Where is Ashley? I need more hands." Ms. Baptiste placed two pies into my hands and pointed me in the direction of the front door.

By the time I opened it, two ladies from the shelter grabbed the two pies from me. I knew then that it was time to get to work. So into the kitchen I went which was where I worked best. We'd baked the pies the night before. Now it was time to prepare the rest of the spread.

Preparation for Ms. Baptiste meant giving one hundred percent of our time and energy. She demanded that everything and everyone was in place at all times. That was the way she was.

"Chop, chop," Ms. Baptiste said as she walked around the house.

Marisol and Amanda, both from Puerto Rico, were busy scrubbing the downstairs restrooms.

Ms. Baptiste walked through the hall. "I still see grime, ladies." I shook my head because she was relentless.

Marisol said," You'd better be glad you're on kitchen duty, chica."

"Hey, more cleaning and no mouthing off." Ms. Baptiste walked by again going in the opposite direction.

"Yes, ma'am," Marisol and Amanda answered in unison.

"That's the way we roll around here," I snickered.

"Morning, Gabby,"Shelira said.

I faked a smile. "Morning Shelira. Ernestine."

"It's about time you drag your lazy butt down here," Ernestine said, tightening her apron strings.

I walked right up on her. "Look, don't start with me today. I'm not in the mood, okay?"

Ernestine rolled her neck. "It doesn't matter to me what kind of mood you're in…" she snapped back.

Ms. Baptiste stepped in just in time. "Ernestine, I'm warning you. None of your games today, do you hear me?"

"I'm not playing," Ernestine mumbled.

"Now Gabby I need you over here with me. This is a very important day and I don't want anything to ruin it. We must beat de iron while it hot" Ms. Baptiste shot a look at Ernestine.

"Yes, ma'am." I smiled a winner's smile and took my place next to Ms. Baptiste at the stove.

When the final cooking was done, we brought the ribs, potato salad, and baked beans outside under the tent. Mr. Williams was busy grilling hotdogs, hamburgers and chicken wings.

Every year Ms. Baptiste would throw this event to raise extra money for the shelter, and as usual, it was a big success. A few big named people in politics gave hefty donations as well as local business owners rented tables to display their merchandise. Uma arrived early so she could help before having to go to work. We talked until it was time for her to leave.

"I wish you could stay longer. It's not fair that Lawrence wouldn't give you the day off." I said.

"The thing is that he wouldn't let both of us off at the same time. But it's okay, you've got important work to do here with Ms. Baptiste."

I shook my head. "I wouldn't say I'm so important though."

"Trust me. I can handle the bakery. You handle this."

About an hour later, I looked up and saw Caleb and Devin coming towards me.

"There's the boy I told you about," I said to Uma.

"And that teacher you don't like, "Uma whispered.

"Yep, that's him," I confirmed as they headed straight for me.

"Hi, Ms. Gabby." Caleb came over and hugged me.

"Hi, Caleb. Hello Devin." I was determined not to let his presence get to me.

"HI, Gabby. It's good to see you," Devin said.

"You too," I said. "This is my co-worker and friend Uma," I said awkwardly.

"Coworker? So you must be a good cook too?"

"Well, I'm pretty handy at the bakery I guess."

"I'm sure you're being as modest as Gabby here. I was blessed to be invited for dinner the other night and it was the best dinner I've had in months," Devin said.

"I could never say that. My mom would kill me." Caleb laughed hard.

Uma laughed too. "Well, it's nice to meet you two. Gabby, I'll see you around." And with that she disappeared into the crowd, leaving me with Devin once again.

Caleb slipped off with the young people and I noticed him playing basketball with some of the boys.

Left alone with Devin, I didn't know what to say. "So… are you having a good time?"

Devin nodded. "So far, yeah. Ms. Baptiste has outdone herself."

"Good." I started slowly moving away from him until I'd left him standing there. I eventually saw him move next to Mr. Williams who was tending the grill. At some point Devin had become the self-appointed game manager, making sure that all games were being played properly.

The DJ played old school music and people danced in the streets. Marisol and Ashley danced with every man in sight while Ms. Baptiste walked around, making sure that everyone was happy. A few of the local politicians showed up and wrote checks for our cause.

Ms. Baptiste walked around, waving her purse in the air. "Gabby, the money is rolling in, sweetheart." It was so nice to see her happy.

My parents arrived after a couple of hours, dressed in semi-formal attire. Why didn't they *just wear casual clothes?* Despite their stiffness, I hoped that they would at least mingle. Hesitantly, I walked over to them.

"Mom, it's good to see you." I said, awkwardly. It had been a while.

Mom grabbed me into a bear hug and I could smell the sweet coconut oil in her hair. She always used it in her hair. "Oh, Gabrielle. I'm so glad to see you." Then she just held me close and stared at me.

I was embarrassed. "Mom, please."

Mom touched my hair. "I haven't seen you in six whole months."

I took a step back. "I probably look the same."

"No, you actually look better." That was mom. She pulled no punches.

"Thanks a lot." I chuckled." I don't know if that's a compliment or an insult."

"It's a compliment," she said.

Dad walked over with two cups of punch. "Gabrielle, good to see you again, baby girl."

I did a quick hug and stepped away. "Hi, Dad."

Dad looked around. "So this is where you've been hiding out for the past two years?"

"No, this is where I've been living." I excused myself because I felt a migraine coming on.

When the DJ started up the music and called for the cha cha sliders, Devin walked over and pulled me in. "Come on, Gabby. Show me some moves."

"Are you kidding me?" I shook my head. "I don't have any moves at all."

"I find that very hard to believe." Devin looked me up and down.

Well believe it." I kicked my foot to prove it. "Never could dance; I've got two left feet."

With that Devin lifted me off the floor and had me almost gliding to the latter part of the dance. Slide to the left; slide to the right echoed in my ears. Devin used his strong hands to guide me and when it was over everyone clapped.

Devin chuckled. "Now that wasn't so bad, was it?"

"No, it wasn't." I straightened the wrinkles from my dress.

When I turned around, I was staring into my parent's frowning faces.

"I want you to meet my parents. Mom and Dad this is Devin Ramos. He's a dedicated teacher and one of the volunteers who helped us put all of this together," I explained.

Mom took his hand and squeezed it. "Oh that's very nice. Good to meet you, Devin."

"Same here, Ma'am, Sir," Devin said.

Dad nodded as he shook Devin's hand.

"It's a pleasure to meet you both but I did nothing really." Devin looked around him. "This is really the sweat of your daughter and all of these lovely ladies here at Home again."

There was a prolonged silence and at that moment, I realized they were ashamed of me, ashamed that I was here, ashamed to be a part of the event. I tapped my foot to stay calm. "Why did you two even bother to come?"

"Because you asked us to come, because we wanted to see you..." Mom tried to smile, softly.

"Then why do you both look so uptight? Like it or not, this is where I live. And this is what we do." I pointed to people dancing and eating. "Now, do you have a problem with that?"

"No, Sweetheart, not if they're taking good care of you." Mom reached out to touch my hair but I moved away.

I started. "No, I take care of myself. Now whether or not it's good care remains to be seen but..."

Devin passed by us. "If you'll excuse me..."

"It was nice meeting you, dear," Mom called out.

"Likewise," Devin said, without looking back.

"See," Mom whispered. "You've embarrassed that young man."

"I don't care about him. He's just some guy that volunteers here sometimes. What I care about is..." Then I sniffed it. "Never mind."

Mommy looked concerned. "What were you going to say?"

I closed my eyes and wished I could start the day over. "It doesn't matter. I should've never invited you two here. It was my mistake."

"Oh, Gabrielle. Don't say that," Mom said.

"I'm sorry but I can't do this," I huffed.

Mom looked confused. "Do what?"

"This whole happy family façade. I can't do it anymore. You're drunk, Dad. I can smell it. Here you all are trying to look so distinguished and you reek of alcohol. And Mom, you know it," I said.

There was pain in Mom's expression. "Gabrielle."

"I don't think you really know how sick that makes me," I whispered. "Please just go."

Mom started, "Gabrielle, we-"

I said, "Thanks for coming."

"Leave her alone, Sadie. Let's go home. She's right; we shouldn't have come down here." Dad took my mother by the hand and walked through the crowd.

I saw them talking to Ms. Baptiste and assumed they were saying goodbye.

I let them leave and felt relieved once they'd driven away. *Too much pain.*

Everything seemed to be happening outside of my control, like I was disconnected from everything. Instead I found a shady spot on the side of the building and kept myself out of sight.

I stayed outside long after the party was over, sitting on the front steps. Eventually, Devin came and sat beside me.

"Thanks for coming," I said. "We really do appreciate all of your help.

"No problem." Devin grinned. "I thought you'd be inside by now. What are you doing out here anyway? A lady like you doesn't belong out here on these streets all alone."

I rolled my eyes at him. "How do you know where I belong?"

Devin paused before speaking. "You're a little feisty aren't you?"

"Some people say that," I said.

Devin threw his head back and laughed out loud. "I hope you don't mind me asking but

how did you get here?"

"I do mind you asking me," I snapped.

Devin chuckled. "You don't seem like you fit in here."

"You're not the first person to say that but I beg to differ. I belong here just as much as

anyone else. I need the same things as everyone else here, a roof over my head, a safe place to sleep, a couple of meals and some clothes to put on my tired body," I spat out.

"That's true but why are you so tired? I'm not trying to pry but I'm just curious…"

I put my hands on my hips. "Why are you so curious?" *The nerve of this guy.*

"Because as much as you put on, you don't act like someone who is down on her luck ," Devin looked at me strangely.

"Really? What am I supposed to look like?"

"I don't know but I've volunteered at quite a few shelters around the city, usually during the holidays..." Devin gestured with his hands. "I've fed the homeless too."

"Well good for you." I signaled with my hands as if I was shouting hooray.

"No, you don't understand. You don't carry yourself like you live here," Devin explained.

"But I do live here. This is the only address I have. There's nowhere else for me to go. And every day I've got to deal with people like you judging me, giving me a hard time or saying I don't fit in." I stood up and started to walk away.

"I didn't mean it like that." Devin blocked me.

"No one ever does," I said.

Devin clasped his hands together in front of him. "I'm sorry. I didn't mean to upset you."

"It's okay. Everyone seems to be upsetting me today. Just mind your own business. That's all." I leaned all of my weight to one leg.

Devin scratched his head. "I can't help feeling that maybe I can help you with something. I don't know what that is though."

"That's your pity talking and I don't want it." I shifted my weight to my other leg. "I'm not a charity case. The truth is I don't need your help. I am perfectly capable of helping myself."

Devin held out his hand but I ignored his peace offering.

Instead I walked up to him and poked him right in the chest. "You asked me why I'm here. I'm here because I want to be here. I need to be here."

"I don't think so. I think you're hiding from something." Devin grabbed my hand. "I'm not sure what it is yet but I can tell that you don't really belong here."

I pulled my hand away. "Why don't you just go home and take your penny philosophies with you?"

"I'm not sure how long it's going to take but I have a feeling that I'll be able to help you."

I picked up an empty paper cup and threw it at him. "Why don't you keep your help and your ideas to yourself?"

Devin walked away. "I'll be praying for you, my sister."

"Don't bother. I don't need your help and I definitely don't need your prayers. The only help I need is this shelter and I won't even need that soon enough."

Immediately, I felt ashamed for the way I was acting. It wasn't like me, but he'd asked for it. *Why does he get under my skin so much?*

TEN

DEVIN

A light breeze blew through the one window in Devin's studio apartment. His curtains were Cheap blue ones and he knew they were probably considered tacky but his aunt had given them to him before she moved to Florida so he refused to give them up; they were sentimental. Thankfully, The open floor plan, if you could call it that, consisted of his sofa bed, a black leather arm chair, the kitchen area which was separated by a half wall. Devin had a folding card table with two folding chairs which is where he ate most of his meals. Then there was a small bathroom with no bathtub, just a shower stall. And his portable laptop desk he placed against the wall next to the door. There wasn't much space but he made it work.

Devin started off his day by praying early; his aunt had taught him that. Today he asked God to bless him with his heart's desire: direction for his career and a companion for a wife. These were the two issues that weighed heavy on his mind these days. Just like Catherine reminded him the other day, he wasn't getting any younger. At forty nine, he needed to make some serious changes and fast.

Devin brushed his teeth and showered before throwing on his teacher's gear, a pair of khakis and a plain blue button down shirt. He looked at himself in the mirror and tried to cover that unforgettable patch of gray that haunted him. In the end, he gave up on the extra grooming, grabbed his briefcase and headed for the door.

He walked a block to the private parking lot that housed his brand new Honda Accord, jumped into it and headed towards one hundred and twenty fifth street. He was moving swiftly at first but as expected, the traffic began to slow down. Bumper to bumper traffic usually didn't bother him; he was used to it. But today he felt irritated for some reason. Oddly enough, he didn't know why.

Once he reached school, his homeroom class was waiting for him. He was one of the more popular teachers and he took some comfort in that. His students even had a "Mr. D." nickname for him. But although he still loved uncovering the mysteries of science, he didn't always agree with many of the Board of Education policies. He often found himself fighting political battles behind the scenes in order to be effective in the classroom. Yes, he was a good teacher. However , Devin had dreams of changing many of the policies and procedures that were in place once he was promoted to an administrative position.

By third period, Devin realized that Caleb was absent from his science class. That was very strange but he continued to teach. In fact, it was unlike Caleb not to let him know if he would not be in class.

At the end of the day Devin saw one of Caleb's friends walking by, and asked, "Hey, Trey, have you seen or heard from Caleb today?"

Trey shook his head. "Nah. Haven't heard from him. His voicemail keeps coming on too."

"Maybe he's sick," Devin suggested.

"Maybe. Or maybe he just stayed home," Trey said.

"Yeah, you're right. I'll check on him once I get home." But his mind was not at ease because Caleb very rarely took time off from school.

Devin walked through the front doors of Harlem High school, still thinking that it was odd that Caleb had missed his class today. Caleb had never missed a day of class since the beginning of the school term. Convinced that an academic scholarship was the way to go, Caleb was excited about science and about the journey to becoming a science professional. As Devin scurried through the parking lot, he wondered if Caleb really was sick.

Once Devin spotted his car, he fiddled around in his pockets for his keys until he felt a warm, soft body press up against him.

"Guess who?" a female said, with her hands over his eyes.

Instantly, he knew who it was. He could smell her perfume. And he instantly regretted leaving the building at this time. Why couldn't he have waited for a few more minutes?

He usually left much later but today he had wanted to handle some business. "Let me guess- Catherine."

Devin pulled her hands down from his eyes and turned around. Sure enough it was Catherine.

"Aww. You're no fun." She put on a mock sad face.

She was dressed in a form fitting sky blue pantsuit that left little to the imagination.

Devin cleared his throat before speaking "How've you been?"

She walked right up to his face and said, "Now, that's the million dollar question because you were supposed to call me to find out, remember?"

Devin snapped his fingers. "Oh, you're right. I'm so sorry but I've been so busy that it slipped my mind."

She put one hand on her curvaceous hip. "Do you mean that I'm not important enough for you to remember?"

"No, not at all. It's just that I've been helping a few students uh and helping out this homeless shelter and uh…"

She flashed her pearly white teeth. "That's very nice, giving back to the community."

Devin had to think fast. "Why don't you come out and help us sometime? We could sure use an extra pair of hands."

Catherine's eyes fluttered. "Hands?"

"Yes, your hands," he said.

"Well, I've been pretty busy myself and so I'll have to see about that." She started slowly backing away.

Devin laughed to himself. "Are you sure because I can come by and pick you up. All you have to do is wear some old clothes."

"Old clothes?"

"Yeah and a head scarf for the …"

Catherine grabbed her weave as if the mere conversation was messing with her hair do. "A head scarf?"

Devin continued, "Yes, the headscarf will protect your hair from the dust."

"Dust? Devin you know I'd really love to help out but I've got to run." She turned on her heels and fled to her car.

Devin called out to her as she approached her car. "So I'll call you then?" He snickered under his breath.

She never turned to face him but merely fanned him away with her hands as she ducked into the driver's seat. "This week is not so good for me. How about I get in touch with you?"

"Cool." Devin chuckled as he slid into his own car.

She started the engine and she was off in seconds.

Devin chuckled, checked his rear view mirror, then pulled out of the parking lot. He turned on his phone to check his messages. He placed his phone on speaker and placed it beside him. He set his radio to his favorite Christian talk radio station as he listened to his messages. There was one from Simon asking him if he wanted to meet up at the gym. There was one from Ms. Baptiste thanking him again for all his help at the shelter. And then there was the one that disturbed him. It sounded like someone was trying to make a collect call from The NYC Detention Center. He didn't know anyone in prison. Then he thought about his more troubled students. There was Daquan who had an uncontrollable temper, who was always getting into it with his stepfather, and Izzy, who at one time was caught bringing edibles to school. He shook his head as he imagined what he would hear next. He continued to listen to the next message. It was Caleb Johnson's mom and she sounded frantic.

He immediately got off the road and parked at a gas station so he could call Ms. Johnson. Devin took the phone off of speaker mode and put the phone to his ear. "Hello, Ms. Johnson. This is Mr. D. I mean Devin Ramos, Caleb's teacher and mentor."

Ms. Johnson's voice wavered. "Oh, thank goodness. I've been waiting for your call. I'm down here at this detention center and I don't know what to do-"

Devin interrupted her. "Okay, okay. Just calm down and tell me what happened."

"They've got Caleb," Ms. Johnson said.

Devin swallowed hard. "Who has Caleb?"

"The police got him." Ms. Johnson let out a little gasp. "He's been locked up."

"He's been arrested?" Devin hit the steering wheel with his fist. "For what?"

"They say he was stealing and they're talking about pressing charges and... I just don't know what to do. I don't have any money and..."

Devin ran his fingers through his hair. "All right now. Don't worry about any of that right now. I'm going to make a few phone calls, then meet you at the jail. Caleb is a minor so he's got to be handled a certain way."

"Please hurry. I'm so scared," she said.

Devin knew he had to be calm. "I'm just leaving school now. I'll be there as soon as I can."

Devin turned off his phone. His heart beat wildly in his chest. He could hardly believe his ears. Had Caleb done something stupid? Surely this was all a big misunderstanding. Either way messing with the NYPD was definitely no small matter. What had he done?

Devin drove back onto the street and sped over to the detention center. He hoped he wouldn't get a speeding ticket himself but he had to get there ASAP.

When Devin arrived there, Ms. Johnson was already pacing outside. Luckily, Devin was able to quickly find a parking space. He jumped out of the car and ran up the front steps.

Ms. Johnson grabbed him by his arm. "Mr. D, I'm so glad you could come. I've been here all alone."

"How is he? I mean tell me what happened?"

"I don't really know a lot. Just that they say he's a thief and that they want to charge him with a felony."

"A felony? What did he try to steal-a car?"

Perspiration poured down Ms. Johnson's face and she trembled as she spoke. "Yes, they say he stole it but he told me he didn't, that the girl…"

Devin interrupted her. "What girl? A girl was involved?"

Ms. Johnson whimpered, "Yes."

Devin put his hand up to his mustache and asked, "Who?"

"The senator's daughter," she said.

And Devin's heart fell.

ELEVEN

DEVIN

The detention center was buzzing with activity all around it. Devin and Ms. Johnson waited for Caleb's paperwork. Finally, Ms. Johnson was taken into another room where Caleb was released to her. Once Caleb was free, they both checked to make sure that he was okay. Thankfully, other than an ankle monitor on his leg, he appeared to be fine.

Devin sat in a chair next to Caleb. "Okay, now slowly tell me exactly what happened?"

"Well, I was hanging out with Victoria, you know, the senator's daughter."

Devin took a deep breath and prepared himself for the story. "How could I forget? Go on."

"So we were just kicking it. Then she told me we could go riding in her father's car. A brand new Range Rover. He'd said he'd be heading out of town for a few days and that his assistant would be dropping him off at the airport. I mean I knew that because he told me that the other day when I was in his office but she reminded me," Caleb explained.

Devin looked puzzled. "Okay, why were you in the senator's office?"

"He'd been giving me a few odd jobs to do and I was hoping to get an internship when I go to college so I've been helping out."

Devin's eyes opened wide. "So you've been working for the senator and dating his daughter?"

"Well, kind of. But not exactly. I don't think he knows I've been dating his daughter."

Devin closed his eyes for a moment to brace himself. "And why wouldn't he know that?"

Caleb looked down. "Because he never approved of me."

Devin shook his head in confusion. "Okay, this doesn't make any sense."

"He let me help him for a week but I overheard him talking to one of his people and I think it was just to keep an eye on me. When Victoria and I started talking and getting close after the banquet, he kind of shut all of that down. I don't think I'm good enough for his daughter in his opinion."

"No kidding," I smirked.

"So anyway I knew that he was going away for a few days and I knew where his car was parked and all of that. And I knew where he kept his spare key just because I happened to see him put it away one day but it was her idea. She knew where his car was parked and everything too."

Devin continued to listen as he tried to process everything. "That's no surprise; that's her father."

"But she's the one who wanted to ride though. And he always parked it there in that same spot and she begged me to get it so we could go for a ride. I told her that I didn't think it was such good idea but she kept on you know… trying to convince me."

"Uh huh." Devin put his hand up to his forehead in frustration. "Then what happened?"

Caleb used his hands to show his driving technique. "Next thing I know I'm at the wheel of her father's Range Rover riding down Madison Avenue. It's about twelve o' clock at night."

"Twelve o' clock. Shouldn't you have been at home? Isn't that past your curfew on a school night?"

Caleb held his head down and stared at the floor. "It was but my mom was working the late shift."

"Of course," Devin said, throwing his hands into the air.

"Victoria already had permission to stay the night at a friend's house so we were both clear. Then all of a sudden twelve rolls up on us. He checks my id and driver's license. Then tells me the car has been reported stolen."

"Stolen?"

"Yep, stolen. Turns out ole boy missed his flight, scheduled another for tomorrow morning and doubled back for the Range Rover. And that's where I come in. He saw it missing, reported it stolen and the rest is history. The police dragged me out of the car, threw me to the pavement face down and cuffed me. Then they brought me here."

Devin shook his head in disbelief. "Just like that?"

Caleb lifted his head. "Yep. Just like that."

"But I don't understand. Where was Victoria when they pulled you over? Didn't she tell them that it was her father's car and that it was her idea for you to drive it?"

Caleb sighed. "See that's where it all gets weird. Victoria wasn't in the car when I got arrested."

"What do you mean she wasn't in the car? Where was she?"

Caleb sat up straight to explain. "She'd asked me to drop her off so she could go in the store and get some snacks."

Devin was disgusted. "Oh great; you've just got to stop at the store at midnight."

"Yeah, I know it was stupid but I let her out of the car and I told her to meet me at the corner when I came back around. So I was circling the block because-

Devin interrupted, "There was no parking."

"Right. I told the police what happened but when they looked for Victoria at the spot we were supposed to meet, she was gone."

Devin asked, "Do you think she got scared and ran?"

Caleb shook his head and looked like he wanted to cry. "I did think that at first but now I don't know cause she told the police she was with her friend all night and had nothing to do with me or her father's car."

"Man-that's messed up." Devin gave Caleb a pat on the back. "Okay, don't worry we'll figure something out. So what's going on now?"

"Well, I couldn't reach my Mom when they picked me up because she was working so they kept me in detention overnight. Then I had an interview with a probation officer first thing this morning. He told me he might be able to adjust my case if I cooperated with him."

"Okay, that's good," Devin said.

"No, it ain't good cause I told him I was already cooperating but no one seems to believe me. He told me he could refer my case to the law department and that the judge had the choice to put me back in detention. I can't do that."

Devin's head began to hurt. "I know. I know."

Caleb pounded on his chair with his fist. "Then my Mom shows up and demands that they get me a lawyer."

"All right. You'll have a court appointed attorney to help with your case, Caleb.

But don't worry; I'll try to make some connections on my end as well." Devin tried to be careful with his words; he didn't want to scare the boy.

Caleb confronted him. "You mean somebody better?"

"Maybe," Devin answered.

"Yeah, I hope so. I heard about these court appointed attorneys from some of my boys," Caleb said.

"You're not *your boys*. You're a good kid with a clean record." Devin put his hand over his mustache. "I'm sure we'll get this whole misunderstanding straightened out."

"I sure hope so. If not I can kiss my chance for a science scholarship next year goodbye."

Devin put up one finger to show his conviction. "It's not over yet."

"It might as well be." Caleb shrugged his shoulders. "I've already been taken to see the judge."

"And?"

"I said I didn't steal a car but the judge said he could've sent me to this alternative school. But he decided to send me home with my mom instead. She had to fill out the paperwork." Caleb held up his skinny leg. "I've got an ankle bracelet like a criminal."

"Well, at least you'll be going home." Devin patted Caleb on the back before standing up. "I've got to go but I'll call you later. Keep your head up."

"I'll try." Caleb sat slumped over in the chair.

Devin walked away from Caleb, feeling quite anxious. He went over to Caleb's mother. "Ms. Johnson, "I'm going to go now but I'll be praying for your son."

"Thanks, Mr. D." Ms. Johnson pointed to a young gentleman standing next to her. "Mr. D this is the lawyer that they sent over, a Mr. Hagler."

"Good to meet you, Mr. Hagler." Devin shook his hand.

"Same here, Sir. You see I wanted Caleb to just make an admission. The judge would've scheduled a deposition hearing and for a first time offender you know…" Mr. Hagler seemed to be lost in his iPad. "I was just asking Ms. Johnson about some of her son's struggles and I was telling her that sometimes the rage within-"

"Excuse me. I'm Caleb's teacher and mentor and I work closely with him every day but I've never noticed any signs of rage at all." Devin took a deep breath. "Just last week he was honored by giving a speech at a senator's dinner which by the way is how this whole mess started."

Mr. Hagler continued to look at his iPad. "I'm aware of that, Mr. D., was it? But sometimes we don't know what goes on in the mind of a teenager. I mean kids these days are-"

Devin thought this statement was ironic since Mr. Hagler, with his pale, petite body, looked like he was barely out of law school himself.

"Pardon me, sir, I don't mean to be rude but I work with *these* kids every day and this is totally out of character for Caleb." Devin tried not to be offended by Mr. Hagler's statements but he was getting heated. "Doesn't his clean record count for something?"

Mr. Hagler finally turned his attention to him. "Well, we'll just have to see about that, won't we? Most of the time the judge will just give them probation."

"You're talking like he's already been tried but what if the kid is innocent? Doesn't he deserve a chance?" Devin was losing patience.

"But he was caught driving the car." Mr. Hagler smirked, then bounced away. "But don't worry, he'll have his chance…"

Devin wasn't satisfied. He whispered, "I'm going to make some phone calls, Ms. Johnson, and see if I can find Caleb *a real attorney*, maybe someone with a little more experience, someone who at least cares about his record."

Ms. Johnson's wig was twisted to the side and her eyes were puffy as if she'd been crying all morning. She looked defeated." Thanks," she said, squeezing Devin's hand.

Devin waved goodbye as he slipped away from the detention center.

Lord, what can I do to help this boy? The first thing he could do was pray and that's exactly what he did.

By the time he arrived at home, Devin was exhausted. He had made his first round of phone calls, putting the word out amongst his colleagues that he had a student who needed legal assistance. Unfortunately, when he did speak to a couple of attorneys, none of them wanted to touch a case involving the senator's daughter. The begging and pleading had made his mouth dry and his soul weary. He needed a friend to talk to about all of this but Simon was teaching his class at the college.

He fell back onto his couch and picked up his cell phone, searching through his contacts. There he saw the number for The Home Again Women's Transitional Shelter and he thought of Gabby. He called to ask if she was available and she was.

Within minutes Devin found himself sitting on the front stoop of Home Again with Gabby sitting next to him.

Gabby sat with her arms folded. "And you wanted to see me again why?"

For a moment Devin wondered why he even bothered to stop by. "Well like I told you on the phone, Caleb is in trouble."

Gabby's eyes looked sympathetic. "What kind of trouble?"

"He was arrested."

Gabby looked him straight in the eyes. "Arrested? When?"

"Last night actually but I just found out a little while ago. His mom called but I was in class." Devin looked down at the steps in front of him. "When I left school and checked my messages there it was."

Gabby looked around both ways. "Let's go inside. There are too many ears out here." She stood up and led the way inside.

Devin followed her in.

Gabby stopped at Ms. Baptiste's office, knocked, then went in. "Come on in."

Devin looked skeptical. "You sure Ms. Baptiste is cool with this?"

"Yes, I'm sure. She shouldn't mind. She went out shopping for a little while but this is the only room in this whole place where there is any privacy. I can promise you that."

"If you say so." Devin came in and sat down in a vinyl guest chair.

Gabby sat in a guest chair right next to his. "What happened? What did he do?"

"Why does everyone assume he did something?"

Gabby touched Devin's hand. "Hey, hey, calm down; we're on the same side where Caleb is concerned, remember?"

"Yeah, I know. I'm sorry. It's just that I had a little run in with a public defender earlier,"

Devin explained.

Gabby leaned in. "So he really is in trouble, huh?"

"Yeah, big trouble," Devin confirmed.

"What is he being accused of?"

Devin sighed. "Stealing a car."

Gabby nodded. "So he denies everything then?"

"Well, not everything because they caught him driving the car." Devin gestured with his hands.

"Aww, man; that's too bad," Gabby said.

"Yeah, he's in real deep and it's a long story but to top it all off, he's all mixed up with the senator's daughter."

Gabby crossed her legs. "The senator's daughter? Oh, I see the problem."

"Yeah and he says she told him he could drive the senator's car and now she's denying everything." Devin slammed his fist against his thigh.

"Typical," Gabby said.

Devin ran his hands through his hair. "I just wish I could help him."

Gabby looked like the wheels in her head were turning. "I'm sure you're already doing what you can to help him."

"I've been calling all around to all of my buddies and nobody wants to touch this case because of the-"

Gabby interrupted, "Political implications."

Devin looked confused. "Yeah; how did you know?"

"It's not rocket science. I'm sure no attorney wants their careers jeopardized for the likes of a precarious teenage boy. Politics is a big deal in New York City."

"It's a big deal in any city," Devin agreed.

Gabby nodded. "So you got there this afternoon and he'd already spent the night at the detention center, so did he tell you anything about his intake interview or whether or not they decided to file a petition. Did he enter a denial?" Gabby grabbed Devin's wrist and checked the time on his watch. "Either way, he must've had his initial court appearance already so what did the judge say?"

Devin never looked up at Gabby. "Well they released him into his mom's custody."

Gabby continued, "With an ankle bracelet and an appointment for a fact finding hearing, of course?"

Devin lifted his head. His eyes grew wide. "Yeah; how did you know that?"

Gabby shrugged her shoulders. "Lucky guess."

"No, really. How did you know all of that?"

Gabby couldn't look into his eyes. "I don't know what you're talking about?"

Devin shook his finger at her. "Yes, you do. You know too much-"

The office door flew open.

"Well, I see you two have made yourself right at home," Ms. Baptiste barked.

"I apologize but Gabby said it wouldn't be a problem." Devin looked directly at Gabby.

Ms. Baptiste looked at Gabby too. "Oh she did, did she?"

"I'm sorry, Ms. Baptiste but we needed to discuss something important and there's no privacy at all and..." Gabby shrugged, remorsefully.

"Next time you find yourself needing to talk privately, take a detour and find yourselves another venue," Ms. Baptiste said, with her Trinidadian accent steadily rising to the surface.

"I'm really embarrassed about this. It will never happen again, I promise," Devin pleaded.

"I know that's right because Mr. Ramos is leaving now." Ms. Baptiste pushed Devin gently toward the door. "I need to have a word with my girls about policies and procedures. Now if you'll excuse me." Ms. Baptiste stood in the doorway of her office and waited for Devin to leave first, then Gabby. "Gabby, you come with me."

Ms. Baptiste opened the front door and cleared her throat. "Good day, Mr. Ramos."

"Again, I'm sorry about the misunderstanding, Ms. Baptiste. Please forgive me." Then Devin turned to Gabby. "We have unfinished business, Gabby."

Gabby shrugged again as Ms. Baptiste closed the front door in his face. "I think we're done for now.

Devin was certain he saw Gabby smile as he was being shut out.

TWELVE

It had been two days since Devin made his way back over to the shelter. During his absence, I figured that he was trying to give Ms. Baptiste enough time to cool off. But the truth was that she really wasn't that upset. He'd just caught her when she was tired and a little cranky but I didn't dare tell him that. I let him go on thinking whatever he was thinking for two whole days of peace. Then he showed up on my door step one afternoon.

Devin was waiting outside. "You can't go on avoiding me forever."

"I can try," I said. "What are you- a stalker?"

"You could but it won't work. And no, I'm not a stalker. Now I'm sure you've seen the news in the past couple of days, talking about how the senator's car was stolen by a teenager. How was that story leaked to the press? Caleb is underage. Even though we haven't heard his name or seen his face, it still isn't right."

"You're right." Now we were having a good conversation the last time we met, before we were interrupted and before I was kicked out. I haven't heard from you since."

I couldn't help but smile. "I've been busy."

"You've been avoiding."

"Whatever," I said.

I tried to get past him but he blocked me.

I put my hand on my hip. "What do you want??"

"Answers," he said.

"Okay."

Devin stood in the middle of the steps. "Okay?"

"What do you want from me?"

He put his hands up to his mouth in a praying fashion. "Please sit down. Just ten minutes."

"Ten minutes." I sat down on the middle step and looked at Devin's watch to note the time.

Devin sat down beside me. "Now my question is about the other day, how did you know all of that information?"

"Know all of what information?"

"You know what I mean-all of that legal information," Devin said.

"Never mind; it's nothing." I tried to brush it off.

"Come on, Gabby."

I shook my head and pretended to be distracted by the noise outside. "It's nothing, nothing important anyway." I looked around me.

"It is to me. You were talking that legalese the other day. You knew exactly what you were talking about too." Devin leaned in to meet me at eye level.

I leaned forward and spoke right into his face. "And how do you know?"

"I just know," Devin leaned forward so much that our noses almost touched.

I backed away, shrugged my shoulders and turned my body to another angle. "So?"

Devin changed positions and kneeled down on the step below me. "So you know a lot about the law?"

"So what?" Again I shrugged my shoulders. *I'm not going to let him break me.* "So do a lot of people I guess. Maybe I watch a lot of court shows."

"No, it's deeper than that. You had to have been a paralegal before or something. No, you couldn't be." Devin stood up and began to pace the step below me. "You knew too much-and don't tell me you used to watch Law and Order either."

"Well, actually that used to be one of my favorite shows," I smirked.

Devin ignored my comment. "I've got it."

"Got what?"

"You went to law school. That's it." He snapped his fingers.

I turned away from him. "You don't know what you're talking about."

"I think I do." Devin turned me around gently. "Did you?"

"Did I what?"

"Oh come on, help me out here a little bit." Devin smacked his forehead in frustration. "Did you go to law school?"

I was silent but I couldn't avoid his eyes. "All right, all right. Yes, I went to New York University Law School. Are you happy now?"

Devin slapped his hands together. "That's amazing."

"Not really." I looked away.

Devin moved his head so that he could see my face. "How long did you go for?" Devin

Now I was annoyed. "I graduated, okay."

"You graduated? So you passed the bar and everything?"

I frowned up my face to show my misery. "You could say that."

Devin looked really surprised now. "So you're a lawyer?"

"Sort of."

"What do you mean sort of? Either you're a lawyer or you're not."

I stood up and walked up two steps. "Hey, hey keep your voice down. I used to be a lawyer. I practiced law for thirteen years." Devin raced up to the step I was standing on. "I don't believe this. You're kidding me?"

I put my hands on my hips. "Nope, I'm not. Now can we change the subject?"

"No way, sister." Devin took me by the arm and led me back to the middle step. "Please."

"I'm not your sister." I loosed myself from his grasp, then sat down.

Devin sat next to me on the step but faced me. "So what kind of law did you practice?"

"I was a juvenile defense attorney," I mumbled.

Devin threw his head back and laughed.

I just peered at him. "What's so funny?

"Now, I know this is a miracle." Devin rubbed his hands together.

"Humph."

Devin looked me straight in the eyes. "Well, were you any good in the court room?"

I closed my eyes and sighed. "I don't know."

Devin smirked, "You don't know?"

"Some said I was one of the best in the city. But others-"

Devin shook his head, smiling. "Yes! God is good."

"Look, I can't be that boy's savior," I snapped.

Devin gently took hold of both my hands. "I'm not asking you to save him; I'm asking you to be his attorney."

I shook my head. "I don't know."

"Why not? What are you afraid of?"

I jumped up and ran up the steps but Devin raced me and won. "I'm not the person I used to be."

Devin stood in front door. "So what? I'm not the same as I used to be. Stuff happens and it changes us, hopefully for the better."

I stood up and walked to the door. "I can't promise you anything."

"You don't have to. Just think about it. Gabby, with the media and the community now turned against him, he's in a very sticky situation. He's got such a promising future and he could lose everything if this doesn't go right."

"I know," she agreed.

"And I believe he's innocent." Devin reached into his pants pocket and pulled out a card.

"I do too."

"This is my information in case you decide to help."

I took the card, then reached for the door.

Devin leaned over, blocking my entrance. "With a public defender he's got no chance at all and no one else is willing to risk their careers to take his case."

"I got it." I bent down to step under his arm. Once I was inside the lobby, I started to slowly walk away.

Devin called out again." You're really all he's got. No pressure but just think about it."

"Right-no pressure." I walked away from the door.

"Young people…" Mr. Williams shook his head and mumbled to himself.

"You're his only chance," I heard Devin say once more before he shut the door.

I wasn't sure why I was here at Devin's' apartment building or what I was doing but something inside just wouldn't let me forget about Caleb. I climbed up to the two flights of stairs and knocked on the corresponding door. It was four o clock in the afternoon and I hoped he was home.

Devin answered the door with a big smile. "Come on in."

I swatted him. "What are you so happy about?"

Devin continued to smile. "I knew you'd change your mind."

"And how did you know that?"

"I just did that's all. I didn't know you were coming by though. I thought you'd call."

"Well, there's no private place to talk at the shelter remember?"

"Right." Devin stared at her.

I made my eyes bulge. "What is it?"

"You don't belong there. That's obvious."

I'd only been there five minutes and he was getting to me already. "How do you know where I belong?"

"Never mind. Are you going to help that boy or not?"

"I'm thinking about it." I rubbed both of my temples with my fingers.

Devin's smile disappeared. "You came all the way over here to tell me that?"

"I'm under a lot of stress because of you and now I'm getting another migraine."

"You're stressed? "Devin pointed at me, then himself. "Because of me?"

"Oh, what do you know?"

Devin stood beside me, leaning his arm against the wall. "I know that you're selfish. You have the opportunity to save that boy's life but you're too concerned about yourself and how you feel. If you don't help him now, he may not get a second chance."

"Well, what about me? What about my second chance?"

Devin lifted my chin and looked into my eyes. "Look, I know what you've gone through and it must've been rough."

I swallowed my spit. "You ain't lying."

"But this isn't about you. I'm sorry but this is bigger than you. God's assignments are always bigger than us."

Now I was really ticked off. "What do you know about God anyway?"

"I know that He's the best thing that ever happened to me; I found that out a long time ago.

People used to always tell me God was good but there's nothing like finding out about that for yourself."

"Oh what do you know? Every time I see you you've got some politician's grin on your face and some happy snappy words like you're running for public office or something. "I started pacing in front of him. "You've probably never been through anything really devastating. Probably had a perfect childhood and everything."

"Actually I did have a happy childhood up-"

"Aha. See, I knew it," I snapped.

"I was happy until my mother passed away from ovarian cancer; I was twelve years old when my aunt and I buried her. That changed everything for me."

I didn't know what to say. "Wow, twelve years old. That must've been terrible. I'm so sorry."

"No, it's okay because even though I had to watch her die a slow painful death, I know she's in a better place." Devin stood up straight. "My mother always taught me to do the right thing even when no one is watching, just because it's right. I hope that you'll consider that when you're making your final decision."

I looked up at him. "Well, I thought about some of the things you said."

"And?"

"And maybe I was wrong about not helping."

Devin's facial expression was serious. "Do you want to help or not?" I put my hands over my head. "It may be too late."

"No, it's never too late." Devin shook his head.

I stared at him. "Where do you get your optimism from?"

Devin smiled. "From the Word of God."

"But how do you know I can handle all or any of this?"

"You can do all things through Christ who strengthens you."

"You're the answer man. Maybe *you* should be in the courtroom," I said.

Devin held up his hand to give me a high five. "Nope, but I'll be cheering you on. My place is in the classroom-not the courtroom."

"I'd have so many things to do. I wouldn't know where to begin."

"I can help. Whatever you need, just let me know. We can do this together." Devin gave me a warm smile.

I paused." A part of me wants to do this more than anything else and yet a part of me wants to run away and hide from the world."

"Let me help you help him. It's time to come out of hiding." Devin reached for my hand.

THIRTEEN

Surprisingly, I let him take my hand as he pulled me into a quick hug. "Thank you," I whispered.

"For what?"

"For forcing me out of hiding." I unpeeled myself from his grasp.

Devin smiled. "Let's start over."

"Yeah, let's do that." I nodded.

Devin grinned and held his arms out wide. "Well, this is it. The great bachelor pad."

I looked around. "It's not so bad."

"You won't hurt my feelings." He made a sad face. "I know it's a dump."

"No, really. I've seen worse." I gave him a fake punch. "Have you forgotten that I'm homeless?"

"Have you seen worse though?"

"I'm an attorney, remember? I've been in a lot worse places," I explained.

I remembered having to walk through a dark alley late one night to meet a client at his tenement apartment in a rough area of Brooklyn. My deceased husband, Barry was so concerned for my safety that he drove me there himself.

"Never thought of it that way, I guess." Devin nodded. "You can sit here at my desk."

I walked over to the makeshift desk and looked at the clutter. "Is this where you sit when you're grading papers?"

"Or when I'm studying." Devin began to clear away some of the papers.

I noticed some of the textbooks he was moving. "What are you studying?"

"Well, I *was* studying for my doctorate in education."

"Really? I didn't realize you were getting a doctorate."

Devin made a funny face. "Why, don't I look scholarly enough?"

"I didn't say that." I grimaced. "Now who is being ridiculous?"

"You're right; I'm ridiculous all day-every day. I'm done with all of my classes though and I've already defended. I'm just waiting for graduation but I don't think I'm going to go."

"Why not? A doctorate is a big accomplishment."

I remembered the day my husband, Barry finished his doctoral studies in analytical chemistry. My in-laws, Teshaun, and I planned a surprise party for him one Friday after work. I'd invited a few of our neighbors, our parents and a few of our closest friends. When Barry came home from work that evening, he wondered why the whole house looked dark. After flipping on the lights downstairs, he was bombarded with balloons, confetti and party horns. I stepped from behind the shadows wearing his favorite party dress, the gold colored, curve hugging one with the plunging neckline. Then I said my congratulations speech before planting a big kiss on him. Everyone clapped as our son pretended to gag. The room was filled with laughter and love. It was such a beautiful night and we were so good together. Now he was gone and there was only an ache left.

My thoughts returned to the present. "By the way, congratulations. You deserve to celebrate."

"Thanks. But it's really not a big deal."

"I don't buy that," I said.

"But seriously, though, I just want to make a real difference in the community." Devin pulled up a chair and turned it backwards before sitting in it. "Now that's important."

"Sounds interesting." I laughed.

Devin smiled. "What's so funny?"

I shook my head. "Nothing."

"No, what is it?"

I started, "It's just that I used to say that exact same thing before..."

"Maybe you can pick up where you left off."

I snapped, "What is that supposed to mean?"

Devin raised both hands in mock surrender. "I don't mean any harm."

"Good because this is not the beginning of anything. I'm just doing a favor for a nice kid. That's all."

Devin leaned over me, neatening his stacks of papers. "Okay, okay. I'm sorry."

I pursed my lips. "You should be. Don't presume to know me. You don't know me."

"Never said I did. I just figured a lady as bright and as beautiful as you are, well you know..."

"No, I don't know," I smirked.

"It's just a waste-that's all."

I snapped again, "I'd like you to keep your opinions to yourself. We're supposed to be working."

Devin stood up. "No problem. I'll stick to the matter at hand-I promise."

"Good," I said.

"I'll get us some coffee," he said.

I watched him from the corner of my eye. "Thanks, that'll be nice."

"I hope you like it with cream and sugar." He winked.

I sucked my teeth.

After a few minutes Devin returned empty handed.

"Well, what about my coffee?"

"It's brewing in the automatic coffee maker. It was a gift from my aunt."

"Oh," I said.

Devin sat down in the chair next to mine. "So what's next?"

"Lucky for you I was forced to renew my license to practice a couple of months ago. In New York State, you've got to renew your license every two years. I didn't want to but in order to get an extension from The Uplift Program, I had to show that I was making progress. Thankfully, I'd saved enough for the renewal fees and I took the required continuing education courses online. I didn't tell anybody though."

"Not even Ms. Baptiste?"

"Well she knew I was taking some online classes but even she didn't know the details. The Uplift Program details are confidential and she respected my privacy enough not to ask."

Devin nodded. "So now that you're all licensed up again and have your first client, what do we do first?

"Well, the first step is to trace Victoria Dawson's steps all week up until the night of the banquet."

"Here is the file of all the information I've gathered so far." Devin placed the file on top of the desk.

"Humph. You wouldn't make a bad paralegal," I said.

Devin smiled. "I hope that's a compliment."

"It is; good paralegals are hard to find," I said.

"Good cause with all of my student loans, I may need a second job."

"I know the feeling." I chuckled.

Devin sighed, before speaking, "I just really wish he'd never gone out that night."

"So do I but unfortunately, it happens all the time," I said.

Devin went over to the coffee maker and returned with two cups of coffee. "I know. A teenager goes somewhere they shouldn't and because of peer pressure and they end up in something they shouldn't be in. I was like that once."

I looked at him. "Really? I can't picture you being a troublesome teenager."

Devin left and returned with our coffee. "Well, I was. The thing was that I was never a follower; I'd find my trouble all on my own. "

I giggled. "That sounds a lot like me."

"Now, I can't picture you in trouble at all."

"Are you kidding me? My brother and I stayed in trouble-nothing big though. Certainly nothing with the law or our parents would've killed us for sure. My parents didn't play that."

"Right."

"Marcus and I were just two rambunctious kids with the whole world in front of us running through Brooklyn.

Devin nodded. "Got it."

I shook my head as I remembered. "But still he and I were like Bonnie and Clyde, always getting into some mess, like breaking curfew, having friends over when we shouldn't have, stuff like that."

"Gotcha," Devin said.

"My parents worked all of the time so we were on our own a lot. My brother is only a year older than me so we were very close."

"Were?"

I took a sip of my coffee. "Yes, Marcus lives all the way across the country in Seattle now with his wife and three kids so you know…"

Devin gulped his coffee. "Yeah, that's pretty far."

"Yep. We used to talk every week even after he moved until two years ago…"

"What exactly happened two years ago?" Devin's curiosity was obvious.

"My whole life fell apart." I began to tremble and reached my hand into my pocket.

"Is that when your husband passed away?"

I nodded my head. "I don't really want to talk about it."

"No problem. I'll just talk about me and how bad I was." Devin stood up and did a silly dance move. "I did a little of everything when I was in high school. I hung with a rough crowd for a while. My aunt ended up raising me by herself and she wasn't home a lot so I had a bunch of free time. And I ended up spending it out on the streets."

"Not good," I said.

"Right. I know that."

"But I wish you knew firsthand the consequences of that. I can't count how many times I had to defend kids who had gotten into trouble after being turned loose on the streets for one reason or another. Usually, it was because of a dysfunctional home environment, but sometimes it was because a single parent had to work, and there was no one home for the child."

Devin seemed to be giving me his undivided attention. "I can imagine."

"The most dangerous hours are always the afterschool hours right before dark. The children do most of their damage during this time, walking the streets, vandalizing, stealing, fighting, and having sex. Not good at all," I reiterated.

"Nope," he agreed.

Interestingly enough, my curiosity peaked. "What turned your life around?"

"Truthfully?"

"Yes."

"I had an older neighbor named Mr. Gregory, a deacon at the neighborhood church who started to spend time with me. He must've been in his sixties then. He started coming down to my school whenever my aunt couldn't come. He came to my games and showed a real interest in me."

Humph, a deacon. "That was nice of him," I said.

"The nicest thing he did for me was introduce me to the Lord. He took me to church with him one day and I thought it would be corny but it wasn't. It was a small church but the next time he mentioned it I wanted to go. I didn't know why but I just did. I got teased by my friends for a while. But it didn't matter; it was almost like I was being drawn. The next thing I knew- I was in."

I nodded my head. "So that's why you became a teacher?"

"Kind of. I always liked science too. But after having that experience I wanted to give back to the kids in the community the same way Mr. Gregory gave to me and other kids in the neighborhood."

I tapped my fingers on the desk. "What ever happened to Mr. Gregory ?"

Devin talked with his hands. "He passed away many years ago but I'll never forget what he did for me. He took me off the streets and he showed me a way to get the streets out of me."

I didn't know what to say after that so I decided to change the subject. I leaned forward and cupped my chin with my hand. "So why didn't you ever marry?"

"I almost did once," he said.

He'd answered but he'd cut it short and for me-that meant that he didn't want to answer. Given my issues, I could certainly understand that. Privacy about my own past had become my mantra. As long as no one knew much, they couldn't ask me questions about it. I could go on living a semi-safe existence, masking my pain and accepting my pseudo reality.

"What about your story?"

"My parents are both city workers. My dad is actually a city bus driver and my mom is a library aide-nothing glamorous. They worked all of the time to keep food on the table for me and my brother. I didn't always appreciate it, though."

Devin chuckled. "Most kids don't."

"One day during the summer before my senior year in high school, my brother got into trouble with the law. He'd been away at summer camp when he and a few of his friends had stolen the camp mascotas a prank. "I punched my hand with my fist. "He'd never been in trouble before but the judge wanted to make an example of him."

Devin made himself rock in the chair. "I know that story."

I stood up and started pacing the floor. "My parents had to scrape together money to get him a good attorney. I still don't think the lawyer did the best job but he got off with probation." I shook my finger in Devin's face. "That's when I became interested in juvenile law."

"Okay, okay." Devin seemed to understand.

Without warning, passion began to rise up in me. "I felt like someone needed to be willing to fight for these kids before the whole rest of their lives were ruined."

Devin was staring. "That sounds very courageous."

"I wouldn't call myself that-just determined." I continued, "My brother and I were the fist in our family to graduate from college. I remembered the day I finished law school and had my parents standing proudly next to me. It was one of the best days of my life. I was so excited about protecting who I considered victims of our legal system."

Devin put his coffee cup down." I can hear the commitment."

I quickly came back to reality. "Yeah but it was stolen from me. When my husband and son died in a car wreck at the hands of a drunk driver. My whole life was shattered, including my career."

"So that's what happened-I'm so sorry." Devin reached out to hug me but I slid away from him.

"Don't be. I don't need your pity."

Devin was silent. He picked up his phone from the desk and started playing around with it. It was obvious that I'd struck a nerve and that he was uncomfortable.

I put my hand on my hip. "You think I'm crazy, don't you?"

Devin answered while still looking at his phone. "No, not at all."

Now I was puzzled. "You don't?"

"Nope." Devin didn't look up.

I tapped him on his arm. "Well, what do you think?"

Finally Devin put his phone down and looked at me. "I think you're scared."

I squinted as I looked into his eyes. "Scared of what?"

"Of living," Devin said, matter of factly. "I think you're scared that if you dare to live that you'll be hurt again. And yet you know that hurt is inevitable"

"Is it? Not if you protect yourself from it, from false hope," I said.

Devin leaned back in the chair again, with his hands behind his head. "So using this gift you have to help people is false hope?"

"You know what I mean. Things can't ever be how they were before. I can't go back." I bit my bottom lip.

"No one expects you to go back into the past. No one expects things to be the same. But things can be different. Things can be good again." Devin reached for my hand but I snatched it away.

I looked at him and rolled my eyes. I wanted to lash out but at the last minute I decided to restrain myself. "Let's just get started with the work. I'll have to set up a meeting with Caleb. And then one with the girl."

Devin shrugged, then picked up his phone again. "No problem. Let's do it."

I studied his arrogance from my peripheral vision and I could tell that working with him was going to get on my last nerve.

FOURTEEN

The sun shined through my window so radiantly that it lit up the whole room. Luckily, I woke up with solutions on my mind. Unlike any other day, today I had a purpose and it was to save Caleb. I stretched before getting out of my bed with the lumpy mattress. Wiping the sleep from my sleep deprived eyes, I showered and dressed quickly; there was no time to waste. Since I did not have to work any hours at the bakery today, nor did I have any in house chores, I was free to work on the case. I looked up at the numbers on the old wall clock out of habit; it displayed 9:00 am.

I knew that I had to meet with Caleb and the girl but something just didn't feel right. I'd been away from the law so long that I hoped everything would come back to me. What would I do? What would I say? What would I wear? That would be a major problem when the time came. Before I could fully take on this case, I had to be ready for court appearances.

Ashley came into the room, "Morning."

I started pulling items out of my chest of drawers. "Good morning. I guess it could be a better morning if I had something decent to wear."

Ashley pounced onto her bed. "What do you need?"

"Well, if I'm going to take on this case which I already have, I'll need something to wear for court appearances."

Wow, I still can't believe you're a lawyer and you never even told me. Like that's so cool. Ashley sprung off of the bed and opened my closet. "Oh, yeah; you're right. And you've got nothing nice in your closet."

"Tell me about it," I said.

"We're about the same size given a couple inches here or there but I don't have anything to loan you that the judge would approve of." Ashley giggled as she held up a strapless dress.

I looked her up and down. "I know that's the truth."

"Look, don't hate." Ashley spun around in her thigh high strapless dress. "Appreciate."

I chuckled. "You're a hot mess."

"Hot is right. I'm sizzling, girl."

I shook my head. "But none of that is helping me solve my problem."

Ashley snapped her fingers. "Why don't we go shopping today?"

I put my hand on my hip. "Shopping with what money?"

"Didn't you just get paid?"

I shook my head as I recalled a glimpse of the clothes I used to own. "Yeah, but not enough for the kind of wardrobe I need."

Ashley jumped onto her bed and stood up. "Are you kidding me? That's because you've never went thrift store shopping."

I rolled my eyes up to the ceiling. "Nope; I haven't."

"Well, you can't be bourgeois and homeless at the same time. It just doesn't work like that."

I looked up at Ashley, straining my neck. "I'm not being bourgeois. I've just never been, never had to. For the past two years I've survived off of whatever people donated. I really didn't care how I looked."

Ashley jumped back down onto the floor and clapped her hands with excitement. "Okay, then it's settled; I'll take you shopping."

"You seem mighty happy for me," I said.

Ashley put her hand on mine. "You know I'd love any excuse to go shopping. It's what I do."

I looked into my closet, doing a necessary assessment. "Well, I'll need dress clothes and shoes. Uma already gave me a pair of pumps since she and I happen to wear the same shoe size."

"Oh that's cool. Uma is your friend from the bakery right??" Ashley snapped her fingers as she was trying to remember."

"Yep. That's my girl. And Ms. Baptiste loaned me an almost new leather briefcase of hers. She said I could use it until the case was over."

"Good; then we're getting it." Ashley grabbed her purse. "Stuff that raggedy wallet in your pocket and let's go."

"Now?"

Ashley clapped her hands together." Now is as good a time as any, ain't it?"

"Yeah, I guess you're right." I looked at myself in the mirror and frowned. "I can't keep walking around like this - not representing Caleb in court."

"Let's go," Ashley pulled me toward the door.

I grabbed my denim wallet off the dresser and we were off.

We walked to the nearest train station, hopped on the number four train and rode downtown a couple of stops.

Then we got off and Ashley took me to several thrift store and consignment shops. "What I need are some designer items for the low low," I said.

"Ain't nothing to it but to do it, girl." Ashley had been in the hood so long I forgot that she was from the Upper East Side.

Our first stop was a little place where I found a couple of suits that I liked. Looking at the price tags, I was amazed that even with my little bakery job, I could afford to shop. While looking through the racks, I found a navy blue Anne Klein skirt Suit with a thin white trim that I absolutely fell in love with.

I held it up in front of me. "Should I get it?"

"You'd be a fool if you don't," Ashley said.

"I never knew that bargains like these existed until now."

"Girl, welcome to the real world."

"I mean back in the day I used to love clearance sales but these prices are even better. Awesome."

Ashley folded her arms and squinted her blue eyes like she was proud.

At the next stop I found a gray Jones New York skirt suit and a black Donna Karen New York pants suit. Then Ashley helped me to find a simple but elegant Forever 21 black dress. My eyes grew wide each time I discovered something new. I also bought a pair of fitted skinny jeans, two plain pastel blouses and a khaki blazer. And I still had a few dollars left over.

With an arm full of bags, I shouted, "Now, I'm ready to face the world."

Ashley nodded in agreement, then held out her hand for a fist bump.

The dilapidated building , with its graffiti filled walls and urine drenched elevators reminded me of the poverty and oppression I faced every day. Devin and I pressed the button for the seventh floor and waited, each of us too sad to say a word.

Devin looked at me. "Are you ready?"

"Sure," I said.

Devin knocked on the door once and Caleb came to the door.

Caleb looked different from the time I'd last seen him; it was obvious that the stress had drained him. "Hi, Ms. Gabby. Mr. D. Come on in."

"Hi, Caleb," I said.

Devin did the male greeting with his hands. "What's up, man?"

"I'm living. That's all I can do right?"

Devin looked very serious. "No, you can do more than just live Caleb. That's why I brought you a *real* attorney."

Caleb scratched his head. "I know you told me this over the phone but could you explain this to me again?"

"Let me do it." I pushed Devin aside and put my hand on Caleb's shoulder. "Caleb, I practiced law as a juvenile defense attorney for thirteen years up until my husband and son died in a very bad car accident. Long story short, I didn't want to practice law any more. In fact, there was a time that I didn't even want to live anymore. But I'm here now because I want you to live and I want you to have a bright future." I glanced over at Devin who had an *I told you so* look on his face. "That's what I went to law school for so, regardless of what happened to me, I figure I owe it to myself and to my community to at least try to help you."

Caleb reached over to hug me. "That's way cool, Ms. Gabby. I never knew…"

"It's okay; no one did." I let him put his arms around me but I didn't squeeze back. He was tall and lanky like Teshaun. "I'm not making you any promises but I'll do my best to help you if you'll help me."

Caleb sat back down and clasped his hands together. "Please; I'll do anything. I can't believe how one night could mess up my entire life."

"If you only knew how many people end up saying that same thing, but we'll work through it.

All I ask is that you be totally honest with me. Believe me there's very little I haven't heard before."

"I ain't gotta lie. I haven't done nothing." Caleb shook his leg as he spoke.

I got right in his face and looked him directly in the eyes. "All right, Caleb. But promise me that even if you had done something, you'd tell me."

Caleb held up his right hand. "I promise. You'd be the *one* person I'd tell."

I studied him for a moment. "Okay. Fair enough." I took out my pad and pen. Now tell me about your relationship with the Dawson's and please don't leave out anything."

"Well, I met the senator at the dinner."

"At the fundraising banquet," I corrected.

"Yeah, you know when I had to give that speech," Caleb said. "And I was so good. That's why I don't understand why all this bad stuff is happening to me."

Devin interjected, "Caleb, sometimes bad things happen to good people. We don't understand everything but it just does."

"Yeah and I thought the senator was a cool dude and everything." Caleb continued moving his leg. "At least I thought he was until I met his daughter."

I looked up from my paper. "And what do you mean by that ? How did you meet her?"

"Somebody introduced her to me and my mom around the middle of the ceremony. I can't remember who but the senator didn't look too happy about it. I didn't really think anything of it at the time but..." Caleb shrugged.

I peered at him, waiting for the truth to break free. "Okay, so what happened next? Did you tell this girl you liked her? Did you ask this girl out on a date?"

"Nah, it didn't exactly work like that. She was kind a coming at me and we were just kicking it. Then she invited me to the back where it was quiet. So I left my mom at the table by herself and we just went to talk some more." Caleb lifted his leg and began to fiddle with his ankle bracelet.

"Focus." I moved his hand from his leg. "So you two just talked?"

"Yeah, we just talked and she told me that she goes to some private school uptown and how she hates it. I felt bad for her you know so I told her about my school and told her maybe she could ask her dad if she could transfer." Caleb's eyes began to wander. "That's when she laughed at me and told me her dad would never let that happen. To tell you the truth, I started to feel like she was a little too much for me but she kinda kept following me around and stuff."

"So you're saying that she approached you first?"

Caleb turned his head sideways. "Yeah, I guess you could say that."

"And this didn't strike you as a little strange?"

"Nah. Girls do it all the time these days, especially at my school. They act really thirsty."

I blinked my eyes fast. "Thirsty?"

"Uh, never mind." Devin waved his hand to indicate that we were moving on.

"Anyway we were talking and then I got up to go back in with the crowd but her dad came up to us."

I leaned in close to him. "And?"

"Well, he didn't really say much but he didn't look happy either." Caleb stood up, then started pacing. "I figured he thought Victoria was too good for somebody like me."

"You mean Victoria?"

"Nah. She didn't act like that. Just her father. "Caleb shook his head. "In fact she was very friendly."

I continued, "What happened after that, Caleb?"

Caleb walked back and forth with an expression of pain on his face. "Nothing much. I just went back inside and later on she put her number in my phone."

It was difficult trying to follow him as he walked but I wanted him to feel comfortable. "Now Devin told me that you were in the senator's office a couple of times. How did that happen?"

Thankfully, he sat down again. "Oh, well when I got back to my table, my mom thought it would be a good idea for me to ask the senator if he needed any help with his campaign. She was trying to get me set up for an internship or something so I did."

I eyed him carefully. "And what did he say?"

"At first he looked at me like he was suspicious or something but when those news cameras came around, when he was asked him about his involvement with youth development, he told them he was very proud of the speech I gave and that I'd be working with him on his campaign for a couple of weeks."

I wrote that down. "And what did you say?"

"I said yeah, cool." Caleb hung his head down for a minute. "I was a little confused but it was all good."

I squinted my eyes. "And what did Victoria say when she found out?"

"She was real cool about it. Said we'd probably get to see each other more often."

I talked to Caleb for a whole hour, soaking up every piece of information from him that I could. It was draining but necessary. By the time Devin and I left, the wheels in my head were already turning.

After law school and during my early reign as a juvenile defense attorney, I'd been hailed as a whiz kid, a bright and rising legal star. I'd managed to obtain a cushy job at an established law firm and moved up each rung of the corporate ladder every year after that. Being able to read my opponent was my calling card, and I used it every chance I got. My supporters used to say I had the gut instincts of a mother panther protecting her young. My critics said I used my legal prowess to finagle the system and to forgive the unforgivable. Either way, something familiar was turning over inside of me.

Before we knew it, we were in Devin's car heading back. It was obvious that he'd waited until we were alone to ask, "What do you think?"

I frowned. "I think it's a mess."

"But do you believe him?"

I turned to face Devin. "I would never have taken the case if I didn't believe he was innocent. I don't know how he got into this or why the girl wouldn't just admit that she was with him that night but someone is hiding something. I need to find out who and why."

Devin looked over at me before pulling out of the parking spot. "So what's next?"

"Next we try to see if I can meet with Victoria. I need to know what she knows. Maybe I can find some holes in her story."

FIFTEEN

The next morning I rose ahead of everyone, working on Caleb's case under my covers until I finally heard Ms. Baptiste and her weekly pick of ladies were headed out to church. I could hear the front door open, then close. I stood up and peeked out at them walking down the street with the four women following Ms. Baptiste like she was a mother duckling.

I ran down the stairs barefoot and went to Ms. Baptiste's office. When I tried to turn the knob, I realized that it was locked. *She didn't forget after all.*

"Hey, hey, what are you doing there, Gabby?" Mr. Williams asked.

"Nothing, Sir. Just trying to get some work done," I said.

"Don't be going in Ms. Baptiste's office. The last time I got in trouble for that. I told her she needs to lock up her office, that I can't be watching everything that goes on around here all the time. Don't have enough eyes for all that." Mr. Williams chuckled.

"I'm sorry. I didn't mean to get you in trouble but I just needed an empty room. It won't happen again." I sighed. "Besides, it's locked anyway."

"What did you need anyway?"

"Just to use the phone, Sir. It's very important. You know I'm working on Caleb Johnson's case."

"Yep, Ms. Baptiste told me. It's a good thing too cause I don't think he'd get a fair shake otherwise." Mr. Williams nodded his gray head. "Every time I see that senator on the news, he looks like he's up to something."

"Well, we'll just see about that," I said.

Mr. Williams reached into his shirt pocket and handed me his phone. "Here, you can use my phone."

I grabbed it. "Thanks. I'll bring it right back." I shook my head on my way up the stairs, seeing that it was a flip phone. I looked through my notes and called like a mad woman for a few minutes. When I was done, I called Devin.

"Good morning," Devin said.

"Hi." I was anxious. "I'm sorry to bother you but I was hoping I could catch you before you get on your way."

"I'm actually just coming in from church; I went to the early morning service today."

I'd never really considered the possibility. "Oh. Do you usually get out so early?"

"Yep, I'm usually an early riser." Devin laughed.

"Okay…great," I said. "Even better."

"What's up?"

I sighed before speaking. "I need you to meet me."

"Meet you where?"

"At Victoria's house. Her parents have agreed to let me speak with her, briefly."

Devin sounded relieved. "Wow, that's good. How did you manage that?"

"I have my ways. Besides, I think the good senator wants it to look like they've got nothing to

hide. Just hurry before they change their minds or something."

"I'm on my way," Devin said.

When Devin arrived, I was already waiting outside.

He hopped out of the car and handed me a small box. "Here, I've got a little surprise for you."

"You didn't have to do that."

"Just open it, please," he said.

I shook it and held it to my ear. "What is it?"

"You'll just have to open it and see." Caleb chuckled.

I opened the box and it was my very own cell phone. I hadn't had one since I threw mine away two years ago. It wasn't the kind of phone I would have chosen, but I was grateful.

"Just a thank you present for helping Caleb. Besides now that you're working on his case, you're really going to need one."

"Thanks. I guess you're right. Communication is pretty important right now." I cleared my throat. "But I'll pay you back as soon as I get my next paycheck from the bakery."

"No problem."

He opened the passenger side door and I jumped into his car. He was still dressed in brown slacks and a tan collared shirt, but he loosened his tie before pulling off. His cologne was intoxicating; I always liked a raw sandalwood scent. Within minutes, we were headed to the upper east side of Manhattan.

Upon arriving at the senator's building, we parked a couple of blocks away, then walked to the building. The doorman allowed us to enter, and after signing ourselves in, he checked to see if Mr. Dawson was ready to meet with us. The doorman pointed to the elevators to the left that led up to the penthouse apartment. I made sure to wear dark shades and a cap because I didn't want to be recognized by anyone. I had once been known in these circles.

Mr. Dawson led us to the formal living room, complete with floor to ceiling wall windows over looking the ocean an elegant wood burning fireplace. The rest of the room was decorated in fine old Victorian style, with marble and other rare stone accents.

Remembering how my own home used to be decorated, I identified with his taste in furnishings.

Victoria was already sitting on the white sofa. As she stood up to greet us, I noticed that she was tall and fit like her father. She had deep brown eyes and long, straightened dark hair that framed her mocha smooth skin. I could see why she caught Caleb's eye.

Mr. Dawson spoke slowly. "Victoria, these are the people I told you about, Ms. McBay and Mr. Ramos. My daughter, Victoria."

"Hello, Victoria," I said.

"Good to meet you Victoria." Devin offered his hand to shake.

"Hi," Victoria said, shaking Devin's hand.

I started to explain the reason for our visit. "Your father was kind enough to agree that we could speak with you for a few minutes. We don't want to take up too much of your time. Like your father said, I'm Gabrielle McBay, Caleb Johnson's attorney and this is Mr. Ramos. He is one of Caleb's teachers and to be clear, most of his students call him Mr. D."

Victoria looked at her "How may I help you, Ma'am?"

"We were just wondering if you knew anything about what happened to Caleb on the night of April 28th."

"Yeah, I do. He stole my father's car. Is that what you're talking about?"

"Not exactly. You see Caleb says that he spent the evening with you and that *you* told him to drive your father's car."

"That's impossible," she said.

I looked up at Senator Dawson who was standing over us. "Believe me we were all teenagers once and I'm sure that all of this may be very intimidating, especially given the circumstances-"

Senator Dawson interrupted. "Excuse me. What circumstances are you referring to?"

I knew I was in the danger zone but I continued. "I'm just saying that if she had gone out with Caleb against your will, then maybe she wouldn't feel comfortable coming forward."

"Trust me, my daughter and I have an open line of communication and I assure you that she knew nothing of this until I told her about it the next morning. Then I had to go and catch my flight." Senator Dawson loosened his collar.

I noticed his firmness. "I see."

Devin added, "We're just trying to get to the bottom of this."

"Then you'd better talk to that hooligan, Caleb Johnson. I gave him a chance to work with me for a few days and he took advantage of my kindness."

"Was it genuine or were you doing it because the news cameras were rolling in order to guarantee votes in the next election?" Devin asked.

"I think we've said enough here. It's clear that my daughter doesn't know anything about what you're talking about and she's already made these statements to the police." Senator Dawson led the way to the front door. "This meeting is over, Mr. D, you say. Good day, Ms. McBay."

The next thing we knew we found ourselves being escorted out of the building by two bald and burly security guards.

Devin stomped to his car, throwing his fists into the air. "What a bonehead. That security escort wasn't necessary."

"Next time just let me do the talking, please," I huffed.

"Sorry. It's just hard to take a guy like that. He's so phony but I can see right through him."

I spoke in my calm but annoyed voice. "So can I but we have to hold onto all our little secrets until our day in court."

"You're right. I apologize for losing my cool." Devin stretched. "What's next?"

I jumped into the front seat as soon as Devin opened the door. "I've got to do some digging into Ms. Victoria Dawson's personal life. I seriously doubt if she's as innocent as she is pretending to be."

"Got that right," Devin agreed as he went around to the driver's side.

I tapped my chin with my finger as I made my plans in my head. "I've got to do some Facebook , Instagram, and Tik Tok snooping?"

Devin checked the rearview mirror, then pulled out of the parking spot. "Is all of that admissible in court?"

"It depends on the details but yes, it can be. If nothing else it can help me gather evidence against them." I pretended to pound a nail with a hammer. "You'd be surprised how many people nail their own coffins with social media."

Devin did a fake cough. "So I've heard."

"The question is why would Victoria deny that she was even with Caleb if she really likes him, knowing the kind of trouble he's in? I mean avoiding being grounded by her parents is one thing but sitting back while Caleb is arrested is another."

Devin tugged on his mustache, something I noticed he liked to do when he was thinking. "Why would she do something like that?"

I tapped my pencil against my notebook. "My instincts tell me there is someone else in the picture."

He kept his hands on the steering wheel but glanced over at me. "What do you mean?"

I snapped my fingers. "What would cause a teenage girl to throw a boyfriend under the bus? Maybe another boyfriend."

"True." Devin nodded as he approached his destination. "Makes a lot of sense."

I nodded. "That's right."

"You're brilliant." Devin parked in front of his apartment building and ran around to open my door.

"Don't get too excited yet. I've still got to piece it all together." I stepped out onto the pavement, closing the door behind me.

"Piece of cake for you, I'm sure." Devin activated his car alarm from his keychain.

"Easy for you to say." I snapped my fingers as I walked towards the front door. "Let's go undercover and find all of their social media accounts and look through them.

Devin unlocked the door and we climbed up the two flights of stairs to Devin's apartment.

Devin looked back at me. As he unlocked his apartment. "So here's a disclaimer. Excuse the mess, please."

I pushed past him and went straight over to the computer. "I'm not here to judge you. I'm here to work."

Devin stood behind me. "What exactly are we checking for?"

"I'm not sure yet. Anything suspicious. When you see it, you'll know. That's how it always is." I clicked on Devin's laptop.

Devin stood next to me and looked over my shoulder. "What if she's already covered her tracks?"

"Trust me young people are not as thorough as you might think. No matter how grown they act, the reality is they're still kids." I tapped myself on the head. "And they still think like kids."

"You're right about that." Devin backed away from the desk.

"Even the best criminals leave clues. They're going to leave loopholes somewhere. I can guarantee it." I began to do my research for the evening, scoping and probing in a way that was all my own.

Devin nodded. "You want a sandwich?"

I shot him a look. "Stay focused, please."

"My bad," he said, backing into the kitchen area.

I made myself frown. "You're pitiful."

"Devin shrugged and disappeared into the kitchen.

When he came back out, he had a sandwich, a bottle of ice tea and chips in his hands. He pulled up a chair, flipped it around and straddled it.

I shook my head as he chomped down the food. "You're pathetic."

"You want some?"

I let out a big breath of air. "You've got to be kidding."

"I know you're superwoman attorney/mega cook and everything, but I'm not bad with a sandwich." Devin pushed the sandwich in my face. "Sure you don't want some?"

"Can you get your mind off of food for a minute? We've got serious work to do. We've got less than thirty days already." I snapped my fingers. "The clock is ticking."

"Gotta take time out to refuel. These chips are the best." Devin continued to stuff his face.

I stood up. "I can't work with you."

"No, forgive me please." Devin gently guided me back into the chair. "I promise I'll behave. My lips are sealed."

"They'd better be because I'm warning you…" I looked at the screen, then asked Devin to log onto Facebook."

Devin leaned over and signed in. "You know a lot about social media for someone who has been in hiding for two years."

"I've been away, not dead. Besides I've followed my shelter mates' social media accounts many times by using the computers at the library. The computers there are free you know? And even when I practiced law full time, I used those tricks." I shook my finger at him.

"Really?"

"Don't be surprised; the police use those tricks too," I said.

Devin threw away his trash, then proceeded to stand over me again.

I could feel him breathing down my neck.

"Would you please sit down? I made my lips make a slurping sound. "You're sucking up all of my air."

"Oh, my bad." Devin moved away from me.

"It's okay; just please relax; here, sit back down." I pulled his chair over to me and patted the seat. "Down."

"Yes, Ma'am," he said.

I started my search of Victoria's account. It was almost clean except for a picture of one questionable looking teenage boy she was hugged up with. He wore jeans that sagged almost to his knees, a doo rag around his head, and multiple tattoo son his arms. He definitely didn't look like someone the senator would approve of. "Bingo." I looked at the date and it was fairly recent. Maybe her dad didn't know about this particular Facebook account.

As a juvenile defense attorney, I'd seen many instances where teens had duplicate social media accounts, one basic for their unsuspecting parents and a real one for their friends. "This may be the dude I've been waiting for …"

Devin chuckled as he stuck another chip into his mouth. "Lowering your standards just a bit aren't you?"

"So funny yet I'm not laughing." I kept a straight face. "Take a look at this guy and see if he looks familiar to you."

Devin leaned in close to the computer. "Nope; never saw him a day in my life."

"I'm going to check her friend's account, the one she claimed she was staying with that night. What was her name again-Sandra? I'm going to see if her friend has this same guy on her page and if so, if there are any comments, any leads at all."

The phone rang and Devin went to answer it. "What's up, Simon.?"

Only hearing one side of the conversation, I could still imagine the rest from the tone.

"Dude, you're kidding me? Two tickets to see The New York Yankees. "Yes!" Devin threw his fist into the air. "Now we're talking."

"Wow, I mean at Yankee Stadium, man." Devin grinned.

I could see the brightness of his teeth across the room.

"Yeah, man. Well, I'm kind of busy right now. No, I'm here working with Ms. McBay. That's right. Why don't you give me a call later?"

I looked back at him. "Why don't you have your friend over if he wants to come over? I can finish this another time."

"Are you kidding me? This is important. Caleb's case is priority," he whispered.

I shrugged my shoulders. "Okay, but I don't want to get in the way. I can work on this at the library tomorrow."

"That's not necessary. Mi casa es su casa." Devin lifted a lock of my hair and smelled it. "Your hair smells so good."

I yawned and stretched. "Devin, thank you and stay focused, please."

"Okay, you're right. I'm losing focus." Devin pointed to me, playfully. "That's why you're the lawyer and I'm just the assistant."

"All right, assistant. Stay with me. So far I've only found one picture of a guy whose history I'd like to trace. I'm checking Sandra's page too." I let my fingers do the working as I scanned the pages, one by one. Then it hit me. "That's it!"

SIXTEEN

As I woke up the next day, I stretched my arms wide, wanting nothing more than to continue my investigation. I'd gone to sleep with Caleb's case on my mind and now I was in full legal mode. It was all coming back to me, every tactic, every strategy I ever used to help any young person I'd ever helped. As I showered and got dressed, I felt a rush of adrenaline flood my body. I knew I had to get it done for Caleb. I had to. I remembered my mother's voice, "Pull it together. Fix it up; everything in its place."

I stopped in the kitchen to speak to Ms. Baptiste who was washing dishes.

I waved. "Good morning, Ms. Baptiste."

"Whoa, whoa, whoa don't just good morning me. Where are you going, young lady?"

"Well, I'm on my way to work at the bakery. Then I've got to make a quick stop at the courthouse before going to the library," I answered.

"So will you be home for dinner?"

"Probably not because I've got to meet Devin after he gets off from work. We're going over the dialogue for Caleb's case today."

Ms. Baptiste squinted her eyes. "Weren't you just working with Devin last night?"

"Yes Ma'am. There's so much to do. You just have no idea."

"I can imagine." Ms. Baptiste smiled. "You and Devin have been spending an awful lot of time together working on Caleb's case."

I nodded. "Yes, and unfortunately, that's what it takes."

"I know that's what it takes for you, the attorney. I just wonder if Mr. D's *only* interest is Caleb."

I shot her a look. "What do you mean by that?"

Ms. Baptiste looked at me over her glasses. "I see the way he looks at you."

I fanned her away with my hands. "That's nonsense. No way is Devin interested in me. I'm sure he's got women falling all over him."

Ms. Baptiste put down the dish she was washing. "And why would you assume that?"

I answered honestly. "Because he's not bad looking, smart, and-"

Ms. Baptiste chuckled. "Sounds like the feelings are mutual then."

"The only mutual feelings that Devin and I have are for that boy that they're trying to send down the prison pipeline. He's such a good kid and to think that going out with the wrong person on that one night could potentially ruin his whole life. That's so ludicrous to me."

Ms. Baptiste dried her hands with a paper towel. "It is sad, dear."

I sat down on the stool at the counter. "I can't just sit around and watch it happen. And Devin feels very strongly about that too. He's one of those teachers who really cares about his students. I didn't have a lot of teachers like that when I was in school. Maybe only one or two that I can recall."

Ms. Baptiste sat down next to me. "I suppose you're right. He's a gem."

I shrugged. "I never said all of that. But he's good with the kids. I guess that's what we have in common. But he's still arrogant and presumptuous."

Ms. Baptiste shook her head. "Funny, I don't see that."

I took an apple out of the fruit bowl and started eating it. "But it's his work with young people that keeps me from taking his head off most of the time. He's really quite the youth advocate."

"You know you need to eat more than an apple."

"Don't worry I'll grab something at work." I looked around the kitchen. "Where is everyone? Why is no one on kitchen duty?"

"Ernestine and Marisol already did their chores here. It's actually Ashley's turn to help in the kitchen but she said she wasn't feeling well."

"Humph," I said.

"What does that mean?"

"Nothing." I put my hand under my chin. "I'm just concerned about her."

"So am I," Ms. Baptiste said. "Her moods have been erratic lately and she's been very secretive about her whereabouts."

I shrugged. "She claims she has a new boyfriend. I hope that's all there is to it but…"

"But what?"

"I know she's been hanging out with the wrong crowd." I tapped my fingers on the countertop. "Well, the other day she dropped something in the room and…I don't want to be a snitch but…"

"Say no more. I thought I smelled something on her clothes the other night but she denied it and became very loud and defensive. You know what they say, a hurt dog will holler."

I took another bite of my apple. "I know."

"I just don't know about that girl. We've done everything to turn her around. The thing is no one can help her until she decides to help herself."

"Sometimes you don't want help because you really don't think you're worth it." I paused. "And when you feel that way you just want to give up."

"That's what I'm most afraid of." Ms. Baptiste dropped her head.

When my shift was over, I stripped out of my black and white uniform and put on my new fitted jeans, lime green blouse and my khaki blazer. As I left the bakery Mrs. Martin gave me her signature hug while

Mr. Martin just stood there staring out of the big glass windows like he usually did, with the gray sky looking back at him. And at that moment I felt his disappointment. I wanted to give him a good pat on the back, to tell him that everything would be all right, but I didn't dare touch him. So I rolled the thoughts around in my head and wondered if they would be considered prayers. *Pray without ceasing. What's happening to me?*

Nevertheless, I said goodbye to Uma, walked up 125th Street, stopped to sample a hot pretzel, licked the chunks of salt on it, and kept on going to the train station. It was a dark overcast day and I hoped to get all of my business taken care of before I got caught in the rain.

Once on the train headed downtown, I had to stand because it was crowded. And I hung on for dear life. People were smashed together , forced into a kind of closeness with other human beings they wouldn't normally be comfortable with. We were face to face, bottom to bottom, flung together strangers sharing personal space in public transportation. But it didn't bother me because I was used to it. Instead of counting down the minutes to my stop, I studied the people, the differences in their faces and voices. It was remarkable how distinct everyone was which is what made being an attorney so interesting to me. Each case was so totally different from the next, even when many of the elements were the same.

I rode in silence as we passed 86th St,59th St,42nd St, and 14th St,. Union Square. The next thing I knew I was at Brooklyn Bridge-City Hall, climbing the stairs, and reaching above ground again, breathing in New York City's smog filled air. I bounced through the crowds quickly, until I reached my destination at 60 Lafayette St. At first glance, the family court building probably looked like any other government building, but the black cube was rumored to look like the "Death Star," which caused it to be nicknamed "Darth Vader". I had been here hundreds of times in past years and the multi-level, oddly designed structure did always seem to have darkness to it. I walked through the glass doors into the building, ready to get Caleb's business handled. Time was slipping away from me.

When I was done with what I'd come for, I packed up my papers and headed toward the front door. For a moment I stood in middle of the lobby, taking in the enormity of the environment. Memories of past clients I'd represented stood out in my mind, some celebrations of victories and some disappointments of defeat. Suddenly, someone tapped me on the shoulder. I inhaled a strong whiff of parfume and hair spray before I heard her high pitched voice.

"So is this the infamous Gabrielle McBay back on the legal scene?"

Although it had been a while, I still recognized her irritating voice. "Yes, I'm back. Hello, Alexis." I whirled around to face her. She hadn't changed. She was still a hardnosed debutante type, complete with big jewelry and big hair to match.

Alexis laughed heartily. "Wow, miracles do happen. I see you've risen from the dead."

I counted to ten on the inside. "I beg your pardon."

"Oh don't beg, sweetheart. It's so unbecoming." Alexis put her manicured fingernail up to her lip as though she was thinking. "Even though after quitting your job and career, I'm sure you've had to do a lot of begging."

I stuffed my papers into my briefcase. "I'm very busy. What do you want?"

Alexis clapped her hands. "Only to congratulate you on making it back, even after two years of being classified missing in action."

I stepped up to her. "There's no law against it, is there?"

"No. No. I can't say that there is one on the books." Alexis circled me like a piranha. "It just makes one wonder what state of mind you were in two years ago when you dropped everything, even your clients, and disappeared. It also makes me wonder what state of mind you're in even now, thinking that you can return to law and just pick up where you left off."

I closed my eyes and took a deep cleansing breath so I could calm down. "Not that it's any of your business but if you'd been following the news you would know that two years ago I lost my entire family, everything that meant anything to me. But I'm not here for you or even myself. I'm here to help this kid."

"You're here to help a kid who stole the senator's car. Same Gabrielle or are you the same? How can we know that your mind is right? Rumor has it that you've been living on the streets of New York City, kind of mentally unstable." She shook her head. "What a shame."

"Look, I don't have to explain myself or prove anything to you, Alexis," I said, firmly.

"No, but you will have to prove yourself in court. And I'll be right there waiting for your fall."

"How can you be so sure that I'm the one who will fall?"

"Well, that's a very good question. Let's see now, you're the one who has been out of practice for two years and you're the one who seems to have had a mental break down in the meantime. Meanwhile, I have been honing my skills like a lion sharpens its teeth before feeding time."

I was getting furious. "I've got something that you'll never have-heart," I huffed.

"Oh, let's stop playing these games shall we? We all know it takes more to win a case than that. But I it will make you feel any better, I'll mention that to the media once you've been devoured. Alexis squealed with fake enthusiasm, "Nice seeing you again, Gabrielle."

When I showed up at Devin's apartment, and knocked on the door, Devin opened the door but spun me around.

"What's wrong?" I started looking around the apartment.

"Nothing." Devin cracked his knuckles. "I thought that maybe we could just hang out this evening. I mean it's Friday and it sounds like you've already had a productive but hard day."

I put a hand on one hip. "You and me? The way we get along? What would make you think that would be okay?"

Devin chuckled. "I don't know. I guess I like to live dangerously."

"Sure." I put up two fists and crouched into a boxing stance.

"No, I'm serious. I think we've both been working so hard and we never get any time for fun. And since you called me to tell me that you now have stalker stress, I figured…"

"Alexis Harvey is like the devil himself. Always has been. Seeing her was like reliving a nightmare." I hit my hand with my fist.

"I'm sorry to hear that but I'm glad you called. While you were on your way over I figured that you deserve to forget about old rivals and have some fun," Devin insisted.

I stood up straight. "What is fun? I think I had the most fun I've had in a while at the festival and that was short lived."

Devin grinned. "Then you're overdue for some serious knee slapping, side splitting fun. I know I am."

I eyed him like a criminal. "What exactly did you have in mind?"

Devin walked out, pulled me along and locked the door. "I've got the perfect thing."

I squinted my eyes at him in skepticism. "Really?"

"Bowling," he spat out.

"Bowling?"

"Yeah, but don't worry ; it'll be totally fair too because I don't bowl either." Devin led the way down the stairs.

When we reached the bottom step, I stood next to him with my folding my arms and tapping my foot. "So you're assuming that because I'm a woman I don't bowl?"

"Oh here we go." Devin dropped his head. "You know I didn't mean it like that."

I stuck my finger into his hard chest and backed him into a corner. "How did you mean it then? Because I could be a bowling champion for all you know."

"Well, I'm not." Devin pointed to himself. "The only sport I actively participate in these days, other than basketball, is cycling and that's on occasion."

I poked him again. "Is that so?"

Devin caught my finger this time. "Yeah, a couple of times a year, I ride through Central Park with my friend, Simon."

I shook my head. "You're off the subject. What about the bowling?"

"What about it? I asked if you wanted to bowl."

"No, you didn't ask me if I wanted to but you assumed I couldn't. And I'll have you know I used to bowl quite a bit."

Devin shook his head. "I should've known."

"And what's that supposed to mean?"

"Nothing at all and good for you." Devin squeezed past me and went through the front door.

"Yep, you're absolutely right it's good for me since some people assume a woman can't play." This time I poked him in the back.

"I never said that," Devin said as he opened the passenger door to his car.

"Humph." I folded my arms.

Devin held the door open. "Is that a yes?"

I sat down in the front seat. "It's a yes and you're on."

"Good." Devin shut the door before going to sit in the driver's seat.

I wasn't sure what kind of time we would have but I was willing to show him that I could bowl. Surely enough after six rounds, four knockouts and no strikes, he admitted that I was a pretty good bowler.

"That's how you're going to knock 'em out in the court room. I can see it now." Devin chuckled.

"Don't try to save yourself now just because you lost." I smiled. "Flattery will get you nowhere."

Devin said, "Maybe I just let you win…"

"Oh come on, you're not really trying the *I let you win* trick are you?

"Okay, okay. To celebrate your bowling win, how about I buy you dinner-nothing fancy. I'll show you my favorite pizza spot. What do you think?"

"Sounds fair."

Once we started walking, Devin tried to put his arm around me, but must've decided against it before I could protest. I wondered what that was all about.

Devin and I sat down to eat the pepperoni pizza he ordered.

"Maybe next time we'll go shoot some hoops. Now that's something I'm good at."

"I'll bet." I took a sip of my peach drink before we left the shop. "Thanks."

"No problem." Devin took consistent gulps of his Sprite.

I didn't know why but I felt like a young girl again. "What if I don't feel like walking back to the car?"

"Must you always be difficult?"

"When I want to be." I started laughing. "Hey, I'm so full; maybe you can roll me back to the car."

Devin started to laugh too. Before I knew it we were both laughing uncontrollably. By the time we'd reached his car, we were practically in tears. Devin reached over and wiped a crumb from my face. For a moment he seemed to be studying me.

But I felt self-conscious. I stopped laughing. "I think I've found something that will help Caleb but I'm not sure yet."

"Cool."

"Maybe you should take me home now," I suggested.

"Why, aren't you having a good time?"

"Because I've got a lot of work to catch up on, remember? And no matter what, I refuse to let that nasty Alexis Harvey be right about me."

SEVENTEEN

The next morning I sat at my desk running through the papers, thinking about Caleb and what I could possibly do to save him. I had worked late into the night with a flashlight under my bed covers. Yet, I had come up with few answers. So far I had a scared kid, a lying girl, and an angry father, who just happened to be a New York State senator. It sounded less like a court case and more like a reality show. Then I had a thug boyfriend whom I had to prove was not only around Victoria, but was on the scene on the night in question. How did she disappear from the scene so fast? Why was she willing to let Caleb go to jail? My instincts told me that she was just using Caleb the whole time. Maybe she was setting him up to take this fall long before the police pulled him over. Maybe she talked Caleb into taking the car so her real boyfriend could ultimately have it. But why? None of it made any sense. But since when did crime start making sense?

I pushed my pencil behind my ear, then leaned back against the wall behind my bed.

Ashley pushed open the door and came in with a laundry basket. "I'm back."

"I'm still working," I said.

"You're always working nowadays but at least you've been smiling a lot more lately," Ashley said. "Does that have anything to do with that handsome dude who you're working with. What is he again, a teacher right?"

"That man you speak of is Devin Ramos, one of Caleb's teachers. But yes, I did have a lot of fun last night."

Ashley plopped down onto the bed. "Where did you go? What did you do?"

I squealed with excitement. "We went bowling. I haven't done that in years."

"Since you've been living here, I'll bet there are a whole bunch of things you haven't done in years. How come you never told me you were a lawyer-*are* a lawyer?"

"It wasn't a part of my life anymore or at least I didn't want it to be. After what I've been through, I'm different."

Ashley bounced on the bed and grabbed her pillow. "But you're back in it now, aren't you?"

"I'm doing this for Caleb because I don't want his life to get messed up just because mine is."

"But you can do so much good and make so much good money." Ashley rubbed her hands together.

I spoke softly. "This may surprise you, Ashley, but it was never about the money."

"I mean you work at a bakery for minimum wage though," Ashley said.

"There was a time in my life that I couldn't handle anything else. I'm still not sure. But I'm going to try my best and do what my gut tells me." Ashley pushed a stick of chewing gum into her mouth. "That's so cool, girl. I wish I was a lawyer."

I shook my finger at her. "No, Ashley, you've got to be yourself and find your own dream. Not mine."

"Yeah, I guess you're right. I definitely couldn't stand going to school for that long- six years. No freaking way."

I laughed. "You just do you."

Ashley sighed. "I will. Just trying to figure out who in the world that *me* is."

"You'll get it together." I smiled at her. "It just takes time."

"Gabby," Ms. Baptiste yelled.

"I'm coming," I yelled. "I'll be right back."

Ashley twisted her lips. "If Ms. Baptiste needs you, don't count on it."

I ran downstairs. Shelira and Ernestine passed me on the way down.

Ernestine stared at me so hard I thought her neck was going to break so I stared back. It was a good thing we didn't both fall down the stairs.

When I reached the bottom, I found Ms. Baptiste standing in the hallway.

"Gabby, you have a guest." Ms. Baptiste smiled and walked away.

I saw Devin standing in the doorway. "Devin, what's going on? Is Caleb okay?"

I stepped outside so Mr. Williams couldn't hear our entire conversation.

Devin took me by the arms. "Yeah, he's fine. It's just that last night did something to me and now I've got to have more…"

I squinted at him. "I beg your pardon."

"F-U-N. More fun."

I put my hand up to my forehead. "Have you lost your mind?"

"Probably," Devin said. "But it's Saturday so I feel entitled…"

I glared at him. "Are you serious?"

"Definitely."Devin grinned. "Will you come with me?"

"Maybe." I searched his face to see if he was tricking me. "Yeah, I guess. Where?"

"Well, it's a beautiful day and I've always loved Coney Island so…"

I couldn't stop the smile that was spreading across my face. "You're kidding, right?"

Devin looked confused. "What? No good?"

I started laughing and couldn't stop.

"What is it? You want to go somewhere else?"

"No. You don't understand." I laughed so hard that my eyes filled up with tears. "Coney Island is like one of my favorite places too. I grew up one train stop away from there."

Devin looked at me hard. "Really?"

I covered my mouth with my hands and nodded. "Really."

"Then what are we waiting for? Let's go." Devin looked as excited as a little child on Christmas morning.

"But what about the work? I'm supposed to be working on the case today."

"Come on," Devin pleaded. "We'll work on it afterwards.

I shot him a look.

"I promise." Devin grabbed my hand and tugged.

"Well, let me get ready. I mean I don't have anything to-"

"Don't worry. We'll stop at the store on the way and pick up a couple of things. My treat. "

"You sure?"

"As hard as you've been working, you deserve it."

I squinted my eyes at him. "Well, I can't argue with that."

So we stopped at a discount store to purchase a few necessities, including a pair of shorts, a sun hat, and a pair of flip flops. With a quick change in the nearest restroom, I was ready to go. Before I knew it, we were riding down 125th Street. Devin whirled through the afternoon traffic, maneuvering his way onto the FDR Drive at Malcolm X Blvd and 132nd St. Then we took Prospect Expressway down to Ocean Pkwy. I could already smell the ocean. Coney Island was on the left. The first thing we saw was the Luna Amusement Park, with its noisy rides decorating the skyline.

Once we'd parked off of Main Street, Devin put the two dollars into the meter. We walked down the board walk to the beach with my heart beginning to beat faster with each step. It happened every time- like magic.

I looked around. "The ocean is beautiful now that we're up close," I took off the flip flops I'd just purchased and sank my feet into the sand.

"I'll bet you haven't done that in a while, huh?"

I was about to agree until I remembered my stop there just a couple of weeks ago. "Actually, I stopped here a few weeks ago on my way to visit my parents." I made a sad face.

"That's all right. I'm sure it'll be more fun with company." With that Devin threw a handful of sand towards me and took off running. I chased him down until he pretended to give up.

I knocked him down to the ground and began punching him.

"Ouch. I surrender," he said, waving one hand.

"Coward." I punched him one last time before standing up.

We went walking through the sand, from one end of the beach to the other, letting the breeze flow through my loose curls and listening to the sounds of the seashore. I collected shells for a little while, stuffing them into my backpack until I acknowledged that I had no place to store all of them and started dumping them all out.

"No, don't do that. Devin grabbed my hand and stopped me. "I'll save them for you."

I looked him in the eyes. "Save them for me until when?"

"You're not going to live at Home Again forever, are you?"

"Actually next month the extension to my program ends." I immediately became defensive. "But that is my business isn't it?"

"I didn't mean it like that, woman. I'm just saying I have faith in you and I'm willing to hold these shells until you have faith in yourself." Devin picked up the scattered seashells and I watched him without ever saying a word.

We must've rode nearly all of the rides in the park, especially the famous Cyclone, which Devin insisted that we ride twice. After that bumpy ride, I was definitely sore all over. Bittersweet memories of how Barry used to complain about the Cyclone every time we went to Coney Island came over me. Devin bought us hamburgers and fries, popcorn and cotton candy. At one point my stomach began to feel queasy. He also bought a funnel cake to take back for Ms. Baptiste.

"Please, no more food. I beg you." I leaned forward, holding my stomach.

Devin's eyes danced with mischief. "Okay, okay. No more. But I see that you've been enjoying yourself, huh?"

"Yeah, too much and now I'm sick. I think I may have to throw up."

"Oh, well the ladies room is over there." Devin pointed in its direction.

"Thanks a lot. This is all your fault. I never eat this much junk food."

"Oh, I'm the king of junk food," he said.

"I see that but how do you not gain a million pounds?"

"The key is moderation. I only splurge once in a while. Believe it or not, I'm no health fanatic or anything but most days it's salads and turkey sandwiches, fruit, Powerade, and water. Oh and I go to the gym to work out."

I hit him with my backpack. "Show off."

He pretended to duck. "Ow. This violence has to stop."

Oh yeah. I'll show you violence." I hit him again and took off running.

Devin caught up with me, lifted me up and spun me around.

Finally, we walked along the boardwalk back towards the car. "Thanks for bringing me here. I had the best time today."

As the sun began to set, the sky turned purple and orange. "Now I know what I've been missing. Fun does still exist."

"Yeah," Devin said.

"I need to get home soon, by ten. Remember?"

"Yeah, you're right." Devin turned around and started to run backwards first, then forward. "Let's hustle."

As we were walking to where we parked Devin's car, we passed a bar. Just then I heard a loud voice coming from the doorway. It was a familiar voice, my father's voice. I turned around to see that it was truly him, sloppy drunk and leaning on two young men.

I couldn't believe my eyes. "Dad?"

"Gabby, what are you doing here?" His speech was slurred and he could hardly stand up.

"I'm just passing by. What are *you* doing here?" Tears streamed down my face.

"Ma'am, do you know this guy?," one young man asked. "he can't drive home."

"I can see that," I spat out.

"Yes, we know him," Devin answered.

Then my father turned his bottle up to his head and began gulping the contents down like it was his one goal in life.

"I think you've had enough of this," I said, snatching the bottle away from him.

Devin helped to hold up my father.

I felt so confused, so ashamed. "Let's get him in the car. Then we can drop him off at home," I instructed.

The two of us managed to get him into the back seat. Dad rolled over and moaned. Then he started coughing uncontrollably and I hoped he wouldn't throw up in Devin's car. We dropped him off at home and never stayed to explain anything. I didn't want to hear any excuses. My mother looked disappointed, as if she was finally ashamed of him but she didn't say anything.

The ride home was silent. There was no laughter, nor joy, nor fun. There was only the sound of my faint heart beating against the backdrop of defeat.

"I'm sorry the evening didn't end well," Devin said.

My heart was so heavy. "It's not your fault my dad is an alcoholic. It's a lost cause."

Devin couldn't let it go. "I wouldn't say that."

"I would," I said, signaling with my eyes that our talk was over. I didn't have time to hear a faith speech.

"You sure you're going to be all right?"

"I'm good. I've been dealing with this for a long time. It's nothing new." I opened my door as soon as he pulled up in front of the shelter.

"I wish I could help," Devin said. "You should've let me get the-"

I slammed the car door behind me. "Goodnight," I whispered, with my eyes full of tears.

It was clear that nothing had changed for me.

EIGHTEEN

DEVIN

Devin went home to sleep but he couldn't. He tossed and he turned in his full sized bed; everything in him was restless. He was worried about Caleb. He wanted to protect Gabby. He wanted to do more for his community. Nothing felt peaceful so he decided to pray.

"Dear Lord, I'm asking you to please help us during our time of need. Please help Caleb not to get discouraged by this incident no matter what the outcome may be. Please clear Gabrielle's mind so that she can defend Caleb to the best of her ability. Please show me what I need to do to help her and to help him. Lord, give Gabby the confidence that she needs to represent Caleb in this case and reawaken the faith that she needs to move forward in her own life. Help her father to overcome his addiction and give the family strength to support him. You know everything Gabby needs on her journey and you are faithful and merciful enough to supply our every need. And Father God please direct me on the path that I should go with my doctorate degree and the many dreams that are in my heart for the future. Help me to fulfill those things according to your will. Thank you, in advance, for your direction, oh mighty God. In the matchless name of Jesus-Amen."

With that Devin grabbed his pillow, fluffed it up, and forced himself to sleep.

The very next morning Devin had an idea. It was Sunday so he called Gabby.

"Morning Gabby," he said.

"Good morning Devin."

"I invited Caleb to visit my church today."

"Okay..."

"Well I was hoping you'd come too. Consider that taking care of the spiritual part of our team."

Gabby sounded cold. "The spiritual part of the team is just fine. Thank you."

Devin refused to give up; he had a strong feeling about this. "Well, I can't make you come."

"That's right you can't ," Gabby snapped. "I want to have a unified team too but I don't like being bullied in this position."

"That's fine. I get it but I'll text you the address to my church in case you change your mind."

Gabby had turned him down right away. His feelings were hurt because he truly felt like their team needed strengthening.

He remembered that he and Gabby had run into a little girl singing, "Amazing Grace" when they were at the beach. Strangely enough, once he decided to approach her, she disappeared in the crowd. He looked in all directions but she was nowhere in sight.

Devin held his arms out wide. "Don't you see that God is running you down?"

Gabby peered at him. "What are you talking about? It was just a little girl singing."

"But *singing* Amazing Grace though?"

"So what?"

"He's chasing after you. He leaves the flock to chase down the one. He always goes after the lost sheep." Devin smiled a big friendly smile. "God wants to bring you back to the fold."

But Gabby didn't smile. "You're crazy."

Devin liked the idea of God chasing after Gabby even if Gabby didn't believe it yet.

NINETEEN

It was Sunday morning again and I watched Ms. Baptiste lead this week's group out to church. I watched them get all dressed up in their best outfits and walk out the front door. After being turned down repeatedly, she didn't even ask me anymore, and that typically didn't bother me at all. She'd just give me that look, the one that usually made me straighten up and take notice. But I never made her any promises. From my window, I watched them walking down the block until I couldn't see them anymore.

I felt more alone than usual but I didn't know what made today different. There was an extra emptiness in the form of an ache. I closed my eyes and let my mind wander back to the night of the car accident. Barry and Teshaun were returning from a fishing trip when the unthinkable happened just a few miles away from my house. I had just talked to them and told them to get home safely. I had just told them that I loved them. And then they were later than they should've been, just enough to make me uncomfortable. I called their cell phones and paced the floor when they didn't answer. Within minutes panic began to set in. Why weren't they answering their phones? There was a charger in the car so their phones could not be dead. So I walked and I wondered and I prayed for their safety. Still, something just didn't feel right. Finally, I got the call from the hospital with a nurse on the line telling me that she was sorry but my husband had died instantly from a head on collision. Then she told me that my son was going into emergency surgery. In less than a minute, everything in my world fell apart. Barry's Jeep Grand Cherokee had been crushed by a speeding truck. Their bodies had been crushed. By the time I reached the hospital, shaking and signing the necessary papers, tired and numb, I fell to my knees and cried out to God with everything that was in me. "Please Lord, don't take my son. That was the last prayer I remembered.

I reached into my drawer and took out my favorite photo of Teshaun and Barry on a boat ride three years ago. They looked so happy together. Surprisingly, the memory didn't make me sad. In fact, I was able to smile through my fresh tears. I was able to think of them during good times. I carefully placed the picture back into the drawer. I went over to my small mirror and dried my face. I could see that there was a light in my eyes that wasn't there before.

Then I remembered Devin's offer to visit his church today. I imagined Devin and Caleb dressed in their Sunday best, sitting on the front pews. I didn't want any part of it. My heart hurt too much to be a part of it. But still there was something different about today. There was a different kind of ache; something was calling me. I paced the floor of my bedroom.

Then Ashley came in "Hey, what's up?" Ashley asked. "Are you crying?

I looked straight in the mirror. "It's nothing. Probably going to work on Caleb's case."

"Right." Ashley rolled her eyes. "I've got a lot of homework to do too."

"Good," I said, looking at my closet but I wasn't listening to Ashley anymore.

"What is it?"

"I'm thinking about trying on one of my new suits." I went to the closet and pulled out the black dress I'd bought during our little thrift store excursion.

"Go for it."

I dressed quickly and slipped my feet into my pumps. "How do I look?" It fit a little snug but it wasn't bad for someone who hadn't had a gym membership in a long time.

"Well, it's not my style but you look very nice." Ashley turned me around so she could get a full view. "What's going on with you?"

I looked up at the clock and realized that there was still time. "I'm going out." I took off my head scarf, letting down my hair and fluffed it out.

Ashley looked at me curiously. "Where are you going?"

"I think I'm going to church."

"But Ms. Baptiste is already gone isn't she?"

"No, I'm going to church with Devin and Caleb."

Ashley twisted her lips. "Oh, that's new."

"I can't explain it but I've got to go." I ran downstairs and didn't stop running until I had reached the bus stop.

Since I was late, I came in quietly and sat on the back row until the end of service. I refused to let the ushers coax me into moving up. I looked around me, admiring the beauty of the mid-sized sanctuary. There were stained glass windows and soft cloth covered pews. Once I settled into my seat, I realized that the senior pastor was a slim older man with a thick gray beard. He preached passionately from the Book of Romans 8:38-39 and his words started to swirl around in my head, words I didn't want to hear. Scripture after scripture, line after line. Was he talking to me? Did he know my background? Did he know I'd been hiding for the past two years? How could he know my heart?" God allows nothing to separate us from his love," he said. Nothing? Even when I've failed him? An usher handed me a Bible and I flipped through it. There were words about love, mercy, and grace. Words that were doing something to me even though I didn't want them to. I remembered my baptism. I remembered Bible study. Then the music started playing and the choir sang, "I Will Sing of The Goodness of God." *All my life you have been faithful...* I remembered that it used to be one of my favorites. But how could it be when he let me down? *Or did I let Him down?* Suddenly, in my mind, I could see pictures of my life, the good and the bad. And I knew that God had been there with me through it all. Even when I rejected him, he still protected me. "Your goodness is running after...is running after me." Before I knew it I was holding up my hands and tears were pouring down my face. It was the altar call and my feet were moving me towards the front. Then I was on my knees. "Father, forgive me...I have sinned against you."

At the end of the service, Devin and Caleb came up to me.

Devin was wearing a dark gray two piece suit. "Were you here the entire time?"

"Not the entire time but long enough to hear the message." I stood up to follow them out of the sanctuary.

"I'm so happy for you," Devin patted me gently on the back.

Caleb, who was dressed in a simple polo shirt and khaki pants, wrapped his arms around me and squeezed. And when I closed my eyes I could see Teshaun. I could feel him too.

"I wish you could've sat with us. Mr. D is really locked in with all of those scriptures. I never knew he was such a Bible scholar."

"Neither did I." Surprised, I looked over at Devin. "I guess I don't know Mr. D. very well at all."

"Why don't you two come back to my place and I'll whip up some lunch for us so we can get to know each other better," Devin said.

"No, I don't trust it. Why don't I make the lunch and Caleb can help? Lasagna maybe."

"Okay so I'll buy the groceries then.

After we arrived back at Devin's apartment, tired and hungry, with two bags full of groceries, I took Caleb into Devin's tiny kitchen; I'd promised to teach him how to cook.

"I don't know about this." Caleb began to giggle like a little boy.

"I used to cook with my son, Teshaun," I said. "So there's nothing to be afraid of. We're going to make lasagna." Together we unloaded the pasta and the sauce, the fresh cheeses and beef, the seasonings, onions and garlic.

Caleb washed his hands and joined me in the chopping of onions and garlic, celery and green peppers. "This ain't so bad."

I smiled at Caleb. "Now we have to pour our mixture into this pan."

"You're good at so many things, Ms. Gabby. You're like a master chef and a great lawyer."

"Thanks, but my mom taught me everything I know about cooking. I don't consider myself a master chef or anything but cooking does relax me sometimes."

"I hardly get any home cooked meals anymore, not with my mom working so hard and so late. When she does finally get home, she's so tired…"

I felt touched. "I know. We'll see what we can do about that. Maybe once a week I can send you a special meal and you can save the leftovers. I'll see how my schedule goes but I'm pretty sure I can squeeze it in somehow."

Caleb grinned. "That would be great. My stomach thanks you right now."

I patted Caleb on the head before sliding the pan into the oven.

Devin walked away from the television. "Don't I get any points for letting you two use my kitchen?"

I shot Devin a look. "Oh come on. You're a big boy."

"A big hungry boy." Devin rubbed his stomach.

"I'll think about it." Gabrielle threw my head back and laughed at Devin's desperation. "I'm surprised you found your way away from the television."

Devin looked over my shoulder. "What are you trying to say?"

I pushed Devin aside to get an oven mitt. "Nothing except that you're in love with a remote."

"And what's wrong with that?" Devin beat on his chest like Tarzan. "I'm a glorified bachelor; I'm supposed to be in love with my remote."

"All right, Devin. If you say so," I said.

When the lasagna was ready they all sat together around Devin's folding card table and enjoyed the meal. It was almost as if we were a family.

I jumped up. "Please excuse me for a moment?"

"Sure," Devin said.

I ran into the small bathroom and poured out my heart. I turned on the water but I was sure that Caleb and Devin could still hear me crying.

I must've stayed in for at least ten minutes, then as I crept out I overheard them talking.

"What's wrong with her?" Caleb asked.

"It's just been a rough two years for her," Devin answered.

"Sorry about that guys," I said softly.

Devin looked serious. "Would you like me to take you home?"

"Not until we enjoy this lasagna. We've worked too hard on it. Well, some of us have anyway." I glared at Devin.

Devin sat back down and picked up the remote. "What? Don't hate. Some of us are culinary artists and some of us are better at tasting."

I shook my head. "Is that so?"

Devin flipped through the channels. "Yeah. I'm afraid that tasting is my specialty."

After eating their special lunch, Devin drove us home. He dropped Caleb off first.

"Tell your mom we said hello," I said, still a little embarrassed about my earlier breakdown.

Caleb waved as he let himself into his building. "I will."

I whispered, "It's a hard life for a teenage boy, staying home all alone every evening."

"I know," Devin agreed as he pulled out of the parallel parking space.

"It's a wonder that he hasn't been in trouble before now." I shook my head.

Devin sighed. "I'm going to do everything I can to make sure that he's occupied from now on so that he doesn't get in trouble again."

"That's quite a responsibility," I said.

Devin sighed. "I have no choice. I don't want him to have to trade that ankle bracelet for a cell."

I nodded.

"I had a bad feeling when he started dating that girl anyway. There was always something about the senator that struck me as evil. I don't know why."

I looked at Devin as he whirled through the dark city streets.

"I can't say that I've ever been a fan. He says he's for the people but I think he's just using us."

TWENTY

That Tuesday afternoon I met with Caleb at his apartment. With Devin at work, it was the only place there was enough privacy. The library would have been too public; we couldn't take any chances. The room had two old cloth couches in it, a matching armchair and a coffee table. Pictures lined the walls, some of which looked like they may have been Caleb's grandparents and one that looked like it could have been his father. I didn't ask.

I plopped down on one of the couches. "So how have you been?"

"I've been okay." Caleb sat in the armchair facing me.

I pulled out my papers and began looking through them. "Devin tells me you've still been doing well in school, at least in his class so that's good."

"I love science and I know it's my way out. I'm not going to mess all of that up because of some baddie who wants to ruin my good name."

"Caleb." I understood his rage but he had to control it.

"I'm sorry, Ms. Gabby. I'm just mad." Caleb knocked a throw pillow off of the chair. "This is so not fair."

I pointed to myself. "But that's why I'm here, to protect those who don't have a voice, to help to balance out the unfair."

"I know I'm but I'm just tired, tired of wearing this ankle bracelet, tired of having people talking about me, whispering behind my back like I'm some criminal or something. Like I'm going around stealing people's cars. But I'm just trying to make it."

I gave him a sympathetic look. "Caleb, no matter what happens, I can promise you this-you will make it. You are stronger than you know. Now let's go over a few important points."

"Okay."

I looked down at my papers again. "The senator and his daughter, Victoria are going to be two of the prosecution's key witnesses. It's my job to take their testimony down."

Caleb looked down at the floor. "How are you going to do that?"

I leaned forward on the couch and crouched down for emphasis. "Watch me. I'm going to point out all of the inconsistencies in her story, things that just don't add up. I'm also going to try to make the senator look like the hypocrite that he is. That's probably going to be the hardest part but it can be done."

"What about me? You still don't want me to testify?"

"No and you don't have to. I feel that it would do more harm than good and I can't take that chance," I said.

Caleb looked confused. "What do you mean?"

I paused before explaining. "My old rival Alexis Harvey is tough and smart; I wouldn't want her to drill you and trip you up. She specializes in getting young people confused, making you say something that you don't really mean. She does a really good job of making the innocent sound guilty. Once she's put that bug in the judge's ear, it's hard to undo so I'd rather you stay off the witness stand."

Caleb looked curious. "How will it work then?"

"I'll speak for you. I can handle Alexis. And by the time I'm finished with her witnesses, they'll be speaking for you too." I reached out to give him a high five.

Caleb gave me the high five, then chuckled. "Is there anyone on our side?"

"Only Devin so far. He's more of a character witness. But I'm still searching."

"Oh," he said.

I put my knuckles against my teeth. "Are you sure there is nothing you've forgotten to tell me? Anything important? Anything at all? We're down to the wire now."

"Well, there is one thing," Caleb started.

"What is it, Caleb?"

He waved his hands in front of him. "But it has nothing to do with the hearing."

"Oh, okay. What is it?"

"I saw your roommate, Ms. Ashley, last night. At first I didn't realize where I knew her from. Then I remembered where I met her; it was at the street festival. I was walking to the store for my mom and…"

"Go on," I said.

"Well, I saw her go into this kind of abandoned building with these goofy looking dudes…"

I didn't dare blink. "Okay…"

"They're known drug dealers in my neighborhood and I just thought you should know, that's all. I figured it's not a safe situation for nobody to be in."

"Thanks, Caleb. You're very perceptive." I put my hand up to my eyes to stop myself from crying. "I'm definitely going to be having a long talk with Ashley." I started rubbing my hands together, nervously. "She does have a drug problem and I'm afraid she's in trouble."

Caleb shrugged, then slumped further down in his chair.

"That's another thing. Posture matters. I need for you to sit up straight when you're in court because even though you're not on the stand, you are on trial. And wear your Easter suit, the one you told me about. Everyone will be watching you, your expressions, your reactions, everything. So I'm going to need you to be mindful of those at all times."

Caleb glared at me like he was disgusted. "So what should I do? Stop breathing?"

"Not completely, no." I shoved him, playfully. "But I do need you to conceal your anger about the situation no matter what they are saying about you. And they will be saying some very harsh things."

"Like what?"

"They'll be saying that you lied, that you conspired, that you stole, that you manipulated, and cheated. You stay calm and let me handle it." I looked him straight in the eyes. "Deal?"

Caleb let out a long breath of air. "Deal."

"All right then, we're good?" I gave Caleb a quick pat on the back before heading for the door.

"We're good," he said.

I left Caleb's apartment shakily, knowing that I had to find Ashley. I started walking down the street and there was a man holding a sign: repent and be baptized. I walked past him without saying a word. *Jesus Christ is the same yesterday, today, and forever.* I stopped for a moment and couldn't move; I felt something moving inside me. I closed my eyes and whispered, "Help me, Jesus." When I arrived at Home Again, Ashley wasn't there. No one had seen her all day and her school called Ms. Baptiste to say she hadn't attended class in days.

"Gal, you've got that look in your eye. What's going on? You know something that you're not telling me."

"No, I'm not sure yet. Just let me check on a lead and then I'll let you know," I said. Ms. Baptiste squinted. "A lead? You're no detective. I hope you're not going to do anything crazy."

"I'm not. I promise. Plus I've got to tell you about my visit to church."

"Church, are you kidding me?" Ms. Baptiste started dancing around the room, clapping her hands.

I hugged her quickly. "But I've got to go now. I'll talk to you later."

I ran outside to use my new cell phone. I called Caleb and asked him the address of the building he had spotted Ashley at the night before. He told me and I wrote it down on a slip of paper in my backpack. Then I started walking in that direction. When I got tired, I hailed a cab; thankfully, I had a few dollars on me.

When the taxi pulled up in front of the building, I immediately knew that Ashley was there. Something inside me knew. "Right here, Sir," I said.

The driver said, "Lady, I hope you're not planning to hang around here by yourself. This is rough territory around here."

"I know but I've got to help a friend," I said.

The taxi driver threw up his hands in mock surrender. "Suit yourself."

I paid him his fare and slid out of the back seat. The second I closed the door, he sped away.

I stared at the brick building straight ahead of me. The windows had been boarded up but the front door was missing altogether. That told me that there had been a takeover. I walked right up to the front where the door should've been but I didn't see anyone at first. Then an old woman came out. She had missing teeth and thin hair but when I looked at her closer, I realized that she wasn't old at all.

"Have you seen a woman named Ashley- long blonde hair?" I said.

"I don't know nothing." The woman tried to get past me.

I got in her face. "I'm just looking for a friend of mine named Ashley."

She looked into my eyes. "Are you an op?"

"No, I'm not the police."

But she had already started walking away in some kind of drug induced daze.

I didn't know exactly what to do but I knew I had to get Ashley out of there. So I went inside and peered around a corner. There was an open apartment door covered with graffiti so I in. Then I heard voices and moaning so I kept following the noises. There was a putrid scent the further in I went. I saw a kitchen stacked with dirty dishes and spoiled food. Garbage was everywhere. Eventually I found the living room where I began to see people, all seemingly in an intoxicated stupor. I could see them but I tried not to let them see me. I scanned the room of zombies for Ashley but I didn't see her right away. There were so many bodies.

Then a grimy looking man spoke, "What you doing here? You looking for a hit, sweetie?"

I jumped, then I turned around. "Oh uh…no…I'm looking for a friend."

"Ain't no friends here, doll. But we can be friends," he said, hovering over me. He pressed me against the wall and put his arm over my head so that I couldn't move. "Now who did you say you were looking for?"

My heart beat like a drum in my chest. "I'm looking for a friend that's all, my friend Ashley Claremont."

The man laughed, then lifted up my chin with his hands. "Ashley huh? Suppose I want to trade you for her?" *Yea, though I walk through the valley of the shadow of death…I will fear no evil.*

"Suppose you want to take your hands off of the lady." Thank goodness, it was Devin.

The man released me and Devin pulled me out of there. He whisked me across the street to his car.

Devin's whole face was red. "What on God's green earth would possess you to go into a place like that? Do you know you could've been raped or killed?"

I threw my arms around him and hugged him tightly. "I was trying to find Ashley."

"I know. I know. Thank God Caleb had enough sense to call me. He had a feeling you were going to do something foolish."

I closed my eyes as I began to calm down. "Thank you. Thank you. I'm sure you saved my life."

"No, God saved your life; I'm just the messenger." Devin held both of my arms. "Are you all right?"

I pointed to the building. "Yes, I am. But…"

He looked over at the building. "Did you see Ashley when you were in there?"

I was still shaking. "No, I didn't but it was so dark and scary and crowded that I…"

"Look let's not go playing undercover cop again, okay?"

"Okay. I'm sorry," I said.

"No, don't apologize. I'm just glad you're okay." Devin hugged me again and his body felt warm.

"We don't know that Ashley is really in there now. And she's a grown woman so we can't bring her out against her will. The most you can do is talk to her about it later."

"You're right. It's just that I started picturing all kinds of things when Caleb told me that she went in there. I guess I overreacted."

"I wouldn't say you overreacted but I think you took the wrong approach. Come on. Let me get you something to eat before I take you home."

"Never mind. I'm not really hungry," I said, solemnly.

"I guess not after your experience. And why didn't you call me?"

I felt so stupid. "Well, I knew that you were just getting off work and I didn't want to bother you."

Devin sighed. "You're never bothering me." As he helped me get into his car, he kissed the top of my head and it felt strange.

By the time Devin dropped me off at home, Ashley was back. I saw her talking to Ms. Baptiste in the kitchen and I confronted her immediately. "And where were you all day?"

Ashley smirked, "Hey, when did that become any of your business?"

"Since I almost got killed looking for you," I snapped back.

Ms. Baptiste came to stand between us. "Gabby, what's going on here?"

Ashley looked confused. "Wait a minute. What are you talking about?"

By this time I was hot. "Your school called and said that you haven't been in class for a few days, then somebody claims to have spotted you in a dangerous neighborhood so I went out to get you."

"Who are you, NYPD?" Ashley pointed to me, then chuckled. "Like really you just went out looking for me like I can't take care of myself?"

I was breathing hard. "You had us all worried."

"Maybe so but no one else was stupid enough to go out into the streets looking for me and then come back and blame me for it," Ashley said.

I looked at Ms. Baptiste. "I'm sorry for blaming you. You're right. I went out on my own."

"You got that right." Ashley looked enraged. "And I don't owe you or anyone else here any explanations about what I am or am not doing."

"It's only because we care," I protested.

"That's truth," Ms. Baptiste confirmed.

Ashley's voice became louder and louder. "Who is we, Gabby? You and Ms. Baptiste. You're probably the only two people on the face of this earth that even knew I was gone. Oh and the stupid school but that's because they want to max out the financial aid money they can get from me. They don't care about me."

Ms. Baptiste looked around at the women who were gathering around the kitchen. "Why don't the two of you calm down and we can discuss this in private."

"That may or may not be true but you've got to care about yourself," I said.

Ashley threw her hand in the air. "And who says I don't?

I pushed past Ms. Baptiste. "Is that new boyfriend of yours a drug dealer?"

Ashley held up her finger. "That's none of your business either."

I continued, "Does he give you drugs and tell you he cares about you in exchange for sex?"

"You've really crossed the line Ms. McBay. Just because you've got your little law career back doesn't mean that you're better than the rest of us." Ashley pointed to all of the surrounding women.

I paid the crowd no attention. "I don't think that at all. But I do think you deserve better."

Ashley took a step forward. "Better than what? Do you think I want to spend the rest of my life in this place with a bunch of crazies and holier than thous interfering in my business?"

I spat out, "Do you call throwing your life down the drain your business?"

"I've had just about enough of your mouth for today." Ashley ran up on me with her fist in the air.

I didn't flinch. "What are you going to do, hit me, kill me? There's nothing you can do to my body that hasn't already been done to my soul."

Ashley made her eyes so small that you could barely see the blue in them. "You're too much for me. All I want is for you to just leave me alone, okay? Just leave me alone. Let me do what I do cause believe me I do *it* really well. Now get out of my face."

I stepped back and let Ashley walk past me. She stomped upstairs.

"Gabby, I..." Ms. Baptiste started.

"Save it. I'm done," I said.

TWENTY-ONE

DEVIN

Devin left school with a lot on his mind. He didn't make any appointments with any of his students and he didn't volunteer for any extracurricular activities. He wanted to go straight home and take a couple of aspirin. He felt a tension headache coming on fast.

The days to the hearing were winding down and all of the preparations had been made. The only thing left for him to do was to wait and to pray. Every day he went on his knees about the situation he was wrapped up in and every day he pleaded about the situations of others.

He sometimes thought of Dana and wondered if he'd done the right thing letting her go years ago. Then he'd reassure himself that she was not the one and that he hadn't even been given a chance to change things. But he was still lonely and getting older so he prepared himself to be happy alone, or at least until the right one came along.

He took a couple of days to be by himself, to reevaluate the direction of his life. He was so busy doing for others that he'd forgotten what he was supposed to be doing for himself. He had to make a plan of action, seek out some new job opportunities, and meet some new people. He'd been so enthralled in Caleb's case that the most exciting place he went to was the women's shelter. He shook his head as he realized how pathetic that was. Simon had warned him about losing himself. Why hadn't he listened? He would've been further along by now if he had. But now he had to start from scratch. He took out his new and improved resume, complete with his new title on it-Dr. Devin Ramos. He had to admit it had a nice ring to it. He wondered if his future wife would like the name Mrs. Dr. Devin Ramos. That was jumping the gun anyhow because he hadn't even been on a real date in months. And the only woman interested in him was pushy Catherine. And no, he wasn't that desperate.

His cell phone rang and he checked the caller ID. It was Simon. His first instinct was to ignore the call and take a long nap. Then he realized that maybe a talk with his good old pal Simon was just what he needed.

It only took Simon about twenty minutes to show up at Devin's front door.

Devin opened the door wide. "What's up, man?"

"What's up, bruh?" Devin and Simon exchanged handshakes at the door.

"Come in. come in. What have you been up to?"

Simon punched the air a couple of times, playfully. "Same old. Same old. Nothing new. What about you?"

"Everything man, but none of it is about me."

Simon looked at him like he was losing his mind. "What do you mean?"

"Well, you remember when I told you I was volunteering down at a women's shelter?"

"Yeah." Simon shook his head. "And I told you that you were crazy then."

"And then I told you how my student got himself in trouble with a Range Rover."

"Yep."

"Well, that's all I've been doing, man, helping this lady at the shelter who happens to be a juvenile defense lawyer."

Simon squinted his eyes. "A lawyer lives at the shelter?"

"It's a long story but yeah-temporarily. Anyway she's helping my student Caleb and I appreciate that so I've been helping her."

Simon put his fist underneath his chin. "Really? And what do you know about the law, my brother?"

Devin sat down on the couch beside his friend. "I've just been doing busy work and kind of being a support system, you know."

"I see." Simon turned sideways so he could face Devin. "What kind of things have you done to help?"

"Well, a few evenings ago Gabby and I went bowling, then Saturday we went to the beach for purely mental health purposes. Then on Sunday the three of us went to church together, then cooked lunch together, but that was only for-"

Simon interrupted, "Spiritual purposes."

Devin snapped his fingers. "You got me."

"And I suppose you've been meeting with this woman frequently, having discussions about the case?"

"You know it. Oh and her name is Gabrielle but we call her Gabby for short, and she's a good cook too."

Simon rubbed his forehead "So she's been cooking for you?"

"Well, no, not for me but for Caleb. She wanted to teach him how to make homemade lasagna and so they came over here to do it." Devin stood up and started to pace.

"Of course." Simon listened intently.

"But I first tasted her cooking when the shelter director, Ms. Baptiste invited me over for dinner, well Caleb and I over for dinner to thank us for our help. Then I tasted her cooking again at the street festival. And that food was really good too."

Simon held up his hand, signaling a halt. "Devin, you're a lost cause."

"What do you mean?"

"You haven't been working; you've been in a relationship. You're spending time with this mystery woman all the time and you're doing all of these family type things together. I mean what's going on here?"

"No, it's really nothing like that." Devin shook his head adamantly as he paced the floor.

"Trust me this woman is not at all interested in a relationship."

"How do you know that?"

"This woman lost her husband two years ago and she's still grieving. I've just been helping her to help Caleb." Devin continued to walk around the furniture. "That's all."

Simon took a deep breath. "All right if you say so but, personally, I think there's more to it than that."

Devin waved his hands. "Forget about me. What about you?"

"I've just been working at the university and working out at the gym. Look at these muscles, man." Simon flexed his muscles. "And I've got a few ladies I'm interested in."

That got Devin's attention. "A few?"

"Yes, I'm narrowing them down as the weeks go by, my brother," Simon answered.

"You need to change."

Simon shook his finger at Devin. "Look, don't judge me. I didn't judge you about your fake family relationship with people who aren't your family."

Devin walked back and forth in front of Simon. "You don't understand. Caleb and Gabby are *good* people."

"I'm sure but that doesn't mean that they're *your* people. I mean either you're in or you're out; that's the way I see it."

As usual Devin used his hands to demonstrate his frustration. "Is everything so black and white with you?"

"Yep, pretty much. I think that if you go out on dates, then you're dating. Call me crazy but that works for me." Simon pulled a Jolly Rancher from his pocket and stuck it in his mouth. He offered Devin one but Devin was too preoccupied to take it.

"But that's not what our relationship is about," Devin protested.

Simon continued to chew his candy. "Okay, then, do me a favor. Tell me what it's about."

"Well, Gabby is smart so we talk a lot. I like bouncing ideas off of her even though she has snappy comebacks. Caleb is a really cool kid and we both care about him. I guess you could say we're both into youth empowerment. And uh that's about it. She's just going through a lot and I like to-"

Simon asked, "Protect her?"

"Yeah." Devin finally took the candy from Simon's hand, peeled off the wrapper and threw it into his mouth.

Simon shook his head. "Dude, whether you realize it or not, you're in over your head."

Devin waved both of his hands to indicate a cut off. "No way."

"How about we make a bet?"

Devin grinned. "You know I don't gamble."

Simon looked at him funny.

"Anymore," Devin added.

"Oh right. Anymore. Well, it doesn't matter anyway because I'm right and no matter what you say, you're gonna owe me... big time."

"You're wrong," Devin chanted.

Simon changed the subject. "So what do you want to do tonight?"

"I don't know."

I think we should go out on the town. Sound good?"

Devin began to yawn. "Nah. I was thinking of turning in early actually."

"Devin, do you hear yourself? You're like an old married couple without the marriage. What are you saying? What are you doing? Let's get out of here. I can make you forget all of this domestication. Believe me, it's a trick of the enemy. "

Devin shook his head adamantly. "You're exaggerating."

"Nope, I'm not. The next thing you know you'll be babysitting and wearing an apron." Simon made mocking gestures towards Devin.

"I am not only a bachelor but I'm bachelor of the year." Devin didn't even sound convincing to himself.

"Oh yeah? Prove it. Go out with me tonight."

"I would if I wasn't so tired." Devin stretched.

"That's because you've been all around New York City with Princess Gabrielle and stuffing yourself with lasagna and stuff. And playing surrogate father to your student. That's why you're so tired."

"Well, you may be right about that. I have been spending a lot of time on other people. I was just thinking that to myself before you called. Maybe you're right about that but I can't go out tonight. "

Simon clasped his hands in front of his mouth. "What about tomorrow night?"

Devin went to look at his wall calendar. "Nah. I'll have to see. We're so close to the hearing date, everything has to be in place."

Simon huffed, "Since you've got it all figured out, what in the world do you need me for?"

"You're my buddy and I'm drowning so I need you to rescue me," Devin pleaded.

"No one can rescue you now; you're too far gone. Night, bruh."

Devin's eyes grew wide. "What? Are you leaving already?"

"There is nothing here for me to stay for. I can't hold your hand and rock you to sleep. And if I stay here any longer listening to this boring life of yours I'm going to put myself to sleep." Simon stood up, walked to the front door, then left.

Devin didn't really know what to make of Simon's observations. Yes, he and Caleb and Gabby had gotten close but that was normal when working on such a serious project together, especially one that you're all passionate about. And he knew that he played the role of Caleb's father in his absence but what else could he do? Ms. Johnson didn't seem to mind the influence he had on her son. So what if he spent his time and energy on Caleb as if he was his own son. What was so wrong with that? He'd taken many students under his wing throughout his career but none of them had ever clung to him quite like Caleb did.

Then there was Gabrielle. They'd started off a little rocky because she was so hard to seal with but that was what made her so interesting and so different than any woman he'd ever met. And although she was strong, he could still see her vulnerable side, the side she tried to hide from the world. Who wouldn't want to protect her? And yes, after hours of talking and sharing and working together, they had become friends. They'd been through so much in the past few weeks. Now they actually had an understanding.

Simon didn't know what he was talking about. Their relationship was innocent enough. And if people didn't understand their bond, then that was okay too because the three of them still had each other. As long as Caleb and Gabby needed him, he'd be there for them. And he felt confident that they'd feel the same way.

He wasn't sure though, what would happen once the hearing was over.

TWENTY-TWO

The next day as I sat in front of Devin's computer, typing away, a mask of depression started to come over me. I'd already been feeling a certain type of way since the incident with my father that night. But suddenly it was affecting my ability to think and to work.

"I don't know how good I'm going to be for Caleb." I turned away from the computer to face Devin who was sitting nearby.

"I guess it's normal to have second thoughts, right? I mean you haven't been in a court room for two whole years. I know you're probably nervous and…"

"It's more than that. I don't think I can really do it anymore. It's not that I'm nervous but I just don't think I have what it takes anymore." I pounded my fist against my thigh in frustration.

Devin walked over and took my fist in his hand. "That's foolishness."

I withdrew my hand and ran it through my curly hair.

As I felt like I was about to hyperventilate, I began to take deep breaths. "That's the truth. I used to have heart back then and I think that used to make the difference."

Devin lifted my chin with his finger. "You have heart now."

"Not like I did though. I used to breath it, live it. My cases used to consume me. I'd be up all hours of the night and I loved it." I closed my eyes for a moment and pictured myself working in the past. "I can't explain it."

"I happen to believe in you," Devin said.

I jumped out of the chair. "You don't know me. You don't know anything about me."

"I know a lot more than you give me credit for. I know you'd given up on life when your family … when uh… when they transitioned.…"

I looked at him. He had no idea what he was saying. No idea what I was feeling or what I'd felt. How my heart all but split in half and disconnected from my body, how even breathing hurt back then.

"I can understand that. I mean I can try. You must've been so traumatized, and…I don't pretend to know the depths of your agony. But what I do know is that God has a purpose for each of our lives and He doesn't give up on us."

I shook my head and gave a sarcastic chuckle. "He must've given up on me a long time ago."

"No, he hasn't."

I looked him straight in the eyes. "How do you know that?"

"Because He doesn't leave us just because we leave him," Devin explained.

"I'm a failure."

"Look, I'm sorry that you had to go through what you went through. If I could take it all away, I would. But I can't. No one can. But that doesn't mean that buried underneath all the pain and all the tears, there isn't a beautiful defense attorney just waiting to be used by God."

"I promise you I'm unusable. I can't do it anymore. When I buried my husband and my son, I also buried myself, my dreams, everything." I walked over to the couch and dropped down on it.

"I know…"

I buried my head in my hands. "No, you can't know. I took everything to that grave and now I'm afraid that I don't have anything left to give."

"You're right I don't know. The problem is you've been stuck for so long. I mean mourning is normal and necessary but I do know that it's just a season. Just like I had to stop mourning my mother when she passed away; it has to end. And I don't know how it's going to end for you but I *do know* it has got to end."

I lifted up my head slightly. "But I keep seeing their faces. The images just won't go away."

"You'll always see their faces in your memories. But just realize they're not being tormented; you are. They're resting in peace. And you need peace."

I wiped the tears from my face. "I don't know how to let go of it."

"Listen to me. I know that there is something inside you. Because ever since I met you, you've been trying to kill it. There's something greater than you that won't die no matter how much you expect it to. It's God's love, his forgiving grace; that's what won't die."

The tears wouldn't stop falling. "I don't know…"

With those words, Devin helped me to stand up and led me to the door. "Come on; let's get out of here and get some fresh air."

We left the building and began walking down the street. "Where are we going?"

"To one of my favorite places?"

I stopped in my tracks. "Now I'm really scared."

"No need to be. It's just a deli up the street about two blocks over." Devin grabbed my arm and pulled me along. "I figured we could both use the exercise."

I loosed my arm from his grasp. "Oh so now you're calling me fat? Great; I'm fat and incompetent."

"No, we've just been working so hard I know we've been neglecting our health and fitness, that's all. I know I have."

"Sure. Tell the fat lady anything." I managed a smile.

Devin chuckled. "You Ms. Gabby, are far from being fat."

Before long we were at the delicatessen. "This is it."

I followed him inside where there were bright red vinyl seats and red vinyl bar stools to match. There was a huge picture of Malcolm X on one wall and a picture equal in size of Dr. King on the other wall.

Devin let me walk in first. "Where do you want to sit?"

"It doesn't matter to me, "I said.

Devin stopped midway. "I must warn you that they serve a mean sandwich in here."

I smiled. "Is that so?"

"Yep. Once you taste it, you'll be hooked for life." Devin continued to lead the way.

I wanted to smile but I couldn't. "I'll take my chances."

"I was hoping you would," he said.

We sat in a corner booth facing each other. Devin and I both ordered grilled chicken sandwiches. The deli was packed with the lunch crowd.

Devin looked around the room. "Well, just a few more days to the trial."

"I haven't been in this position in a long time; it's scary."

"I know," Devin said.

"But I feel like it's Caleb's only shot. At the same time, I'm scared, I'm excited. And I have you to thank for that and to blame for that." I leaned forward and looked into his deep brown eyes. Suddenly, I felt drawn to him. My feelings shocked me and I immediately leaned back in my seat.

"I haven't done anything. You cared enough about Caleb to put your personal issues aside and defend him." Devin took my hand in his and squeezed. "For that I should be thanking you over and over again."

"I just don't want that kid's life to be ruined. That's the whole reason I became a juvenile defense attorney in the first place. It's a tough case though so I don't know how it's all going to play out." My eyes caught his again and I pulled my hand away from his.

Devin's gaze seemed magnetic. "I'm sure it'll be okay. There's always a ram in the bush."

Now he sounded like Ms. Baptiste.

I nodded in silence as Devin pushed a curly lock from my face.

I closed my eyes to absorb the moment. Just then I heard footsteps- the sound of stiletto heels. When I opened my eyes, my nightmare began.

"Devin Ramos, is that you?" the woman said.

She was tall and beautiful, with waist long ginger colored weave, and long, shapely legs, the model type. She was wearing a tennis outfit with matching sneakers and I wondered if she really played tennis. There was a tall boy standing next to her.

Devin peered at her curiously, without moving at first. "Dana?"

"Of course." She leaned in for a hug. "Long time no see."

"You could say that." Devin looked visibly shaken but he hugged her quickly.

Devin asked, "What are you doing here in New York City?"

"We're in town for a film festival," she said. "I'm sorry. This is my son Jared." The woman patted the boy on the head.

Devin raised his eyebrows. "Your son?"

"Yes. Say hi, Jared," she said.

Jared said, "Hi."

She looked directly at me. "Aren't you going to introduce me to your lady friend?"

"Oh, yes, Gabrielle this is Dana. We used to be very close," Devin explained, while maintaining eye contact with Dana. "And Dana this is Gabrielle McBay. She's an attorney and she's helping me defend one of my students who got into some trouble."

"Oh, that's too bad." She reached into her purse and retrieved a business card. "Good thing he has good representation though. Nice to meet you, ma'am." She held out her hand.

Ma'am? I took her hand and barely shook it. "The pleasure is all mine." *How old does she think I am?*

Devin couldn't take his eyes off of the boy. "How old did you say your son was?"

"He's ten years old." Dana looked down at her son and smiled.

There was a moment of silence and then Dana's phone rang.

Dana looked at her cell phone, then before she answered it, said, "I've got to take this important call but maybe we can get together sometime soon and catch up." Within seconds she had slipped him her card and left the building with the phone still glued to her ear.

I sat up straight in my chair. "What was that hurricane all about?"

Devin took a sip of his lemonade. "Just an old girlfriend."

"Oh, I see." Suddenly, I felt very self-conscious. "She's gorgeous."

"If you like the flashy type-yeah," he agreed.

"How long has it been?"

"That's what I was just thinking about actually." Devin looked stunned. "A little over eight years maybe."

We stared at each other for a few minutes, exchanging no words. It was too awkward.

"Why don't you just ask her? It's obvious that it's on your mind," I blurted out.

"I just wonder how, when? And why she never told me she was pregnant or maybe I'm calculating something wrong. "

"Maybe the boy is adopted," I suggested.

"Nah; she's not the adopting type."

I nodded. "Well, you'd know."

"I don't think I know anything anymore. One minute my life made perfect sense and the next minute everything is out of order."

I tried to sound lighthearted. "You don't think she'd actually keep a son from you all these years do you?"

Devin put his head in his hands. "I don't know. I just don't."

"If she did, how would you feel about being a father?"

"That's not such a bad thing but I would've wanted more time with him. I would've missed so much of his life. I mean I don't know him at all." Devin put his hand on his forehead.

"I guess you'll have to call her to find out." I drummed my fingers on the table. "You have her card."

Devin looked as if his mind was far away. "Yeah, I think I'll have to call her."

I bit my lip. "She must've been pretty important to you…?"

"Remember when you asked me why I never married? Dana and I were engaged until she up and moved to LA."

I sucked down the last of my sweet tea. "Oh wow. That's horrible."

Devin nodded. "Yep broke up with me with no explanation."

"Well, personally, I don't know how you could've not asked her," I said.

"What are you talking about? I was heartbroken and I wasn't thinking straight."

"I guess not," I snapped.

Devin explained, "I had a lot going on back then and so did she."

"I still don't know how you could've missed something as obvious as a pregnancy. I mean that's pretty big you know?"

"I can't believe you."

I pointed to myself. "Can't believe me ?"

Devin's light complexion was quickly turning tomato red. "Are you that insensitive right now that you're sitting here grilling me about how I didn't notice my ex-girlfriend was pregnant? Are you calling me stupid?"

"That's not what I'm saying. And you don't have to start acting all brand new." Gabby threw her hands in the air. "I just figured that you'd see some of the signs or something."

"Signs? Signs?" Devin became more and more flustered. "You know what? Never mind. Forget it."

"Fine," Gabby said.

Devin threw his napkin down on the table. "In fact, forget it"

Gabby rolled her eyes. "Not if I forget it first."

"I've got enough issues. I don't have to deal with this nonsense." Devin stood up, threw a wad of cash on the table and walked out.

TWENTY-THREE

DEVIN

Devin strolled over to the door, fully expecting it to be Simon. He'd called earlier to say that he might be stopping by. When he asked who it was, however, he was surprised by the familiar woman's voice. Confused, he pulled open the door to see Dana standing in the doorway.

"Hi, Devin," Dana said.

Devin took a deep breath. "Hi."

Dana peeked into the apartment. "Well, aren't you going to invite me in?"

"Yes, please come in." Devin stood back and signaled the way in.

Dana walked by him, wearing a short, form fitting, backless dress. It was pale pink and it matched with her pale pink stiletto sandals. He took in her provocative scent as she passed by.

Once he had closed the door, he walked over to where she was standing. "What are you doing here?"

"You left me a voicemail." Dana didn't blink.

Devin's tone was dry. "That was two days ago."

"I'm sorry but it took me a while," she answered.

Devin looked her straight in the eyes. "I understand if your schedule-"

"No, not my schedule-my conscience." Dana looked down.

Devin felt a pit in his stomach.

Dana looked back at the couch behind her, then sat down. Once she had placed her purse beside her, she crossed her long, perfectly shaped legs. In fact, she crossed her legs, revealing a big chunk of thigh. He noticed that her toenails and fingernails were both painted gold and pink also. She was one of the most beautiful women he had ever known, which was why he was so easily mesmerized by her years ago.

Devin continued to face her, staring.

"When you saw me at the cafe with my son and I told you that he was ten, that was really hard for me," she started.

Devin sighed. "Maybe I'd better sit down too." He clumsily found his way to the couch in front of him.

"Yes, please." Dana continued, "I looked into your eyes and I saw confusion and pain but I came to clear it all up."

Devin stared at her blankly. He didn't dare move or say a word.

"Look, we broke up almost nine years ago and you're a smart man so I'm sure you've already done the math." Dana paused to put her face in her hands, pushing back her long curly locks. "I was having a really hard time with my career and all…."

"I remember that," Devin confirmed.

"It wasn't the easiest game to play back then; it still isn't. And all I ever wanted was to be let in the Hollywood game, you know." She fluttered her fake eyelashes.

Devin remembered her struggles as an up and coming actress and felt compassion for her. "I know."

"That's really all I wanted –just a fair shot. Anyway, there was this dude, a pretty big time director, whose name isn't important now, but he told me all the things I wanted to hear. He promised me the world or at least a good part of it. Dana closed her eyes and a single tear burst through. "I was waiting on that leading role and he promised to make me a star."

Devin began to sense what she was about to say. "And you fell for it?"

"Yeah, I did and I regret it." Dana grabbed Devin's hand and held it tight. "I wanted so much for it to be true." I wanted something that was bigger than me. I can't explain it but have you ever wanted something that was so out of your league?"

"Yep." Devin swallowed hard and pulled his hand away from hers.

"But I'm glad I ran into you the other day because I always wanted to explain." She dried her face with her hand.

Devin put his hand up to his budding beard and began to nervously scratch his chin. "So let me understand this, you had me thinking that you left me because you were in love with your career but all the while it was another man?"

Dana leaned her voluptuous body forward. "No, I was in love with my career most of all."

A part of him made Devin want to explode. "But you could've told me that before we made wedding plans you know."

"I know," she said.

Devin cleared his throat. "Not that it matters now but did you love him?"

"No."

Devin shook his head as he processed this new information. "I mean you and I were in a relationship for a year, then engaged for six months."

Dana spoke in a soft voice through her pink colored lips. "I know and believe me I'm sorry about that."

"Are you?"

Dana rolled her eyes up to the ceiling. "I didn't come here to get into it with you, Devin. We've been down that road before, remember?"

"How did you expect me to react?" Devin's mind went back to their on again, off again, often tumultuous situationship. In seconds of silence, he remembered the obsession, the passion, and the pain.

"I'm not sure what I expected," Dana said with pouting lips.

Despite his best attempts, was losing patience. "Why did you come?"

"To let you know that Jared is not your son. I had to tell you that in case you suspected that he was."

A wave of disappointment showered over him. "No, I've got it now." Devin closed his eyes to shut out what could never be.

"Again, I'm sorry. He should've been yours." Dana stood up.

"It's okay." Devin opened the door and held it for her. "God has blessed you with a healthy and strong son; take good care of him."

Dana looked remorseful as she stepped into the hallway. "Devin, I…"

"It's okay, I'm a new man now. Jesus got a hold of me a couple of years ago and turned my life upside down." Devin stood beside her and forced a smile. "Don't worry about me. The best is yet to come."

Dana nodded in silence.

"I guess it just wasn't meant to be," Devin said, trying to mask his disappointment.

"I guess not," she agreed.

"Take care of yourself."

"You too," Dana touched his lips with two of her finely manicured fingers before walking away.

Devin closed the door behind her but stood against the door for a moment, absorbing the details of their conversation. So he wasn't a father after all. She had cheated on him with another man and found herself pregnant during their engagement. That certainly explained her abrupt departure. He'd loved her once. Devin began to pace the room, wondering if she'd been honest with him if he would've taken the child to raise as his own. It was too late for that now, of course, but she'd never even given him the chance. He wasn't even sure he could've handled the truth if she had told him; he was so immature back then. In any case, he would never know the answer to that question.

Surprisingly, he wasn't sad anymore; she no longer had the same effect on him. He walked over to his desk and sat down. It had been a long day and he felt exhausted. Since tomorrow was the start of the fact finding hearing, he knew he had to get some rest soon if he was going to be the most effective in helping Caleb. When he looked at the time, however, it was still only eight o'clock. Too early for a grown man to go to bed he thought.

He looked at the pile of notes that Gabby had left for him and began to read over them one last time. He was certain that Gabrielle was hard at work on Caleb's case, although he hadn't heard from her since their argument two days ago. Devin knew she was as passionate as he was about saving Caleb. He'd tried to call her the day before and left two voicemails on her cell and messages with Ms. Baptiste but she wouldn't return his calls. He'd hoped that a few days away from each other would ease their differences.

Then he decided to turn on his computer and found himself glaring at its screen. First he checked his email which was filled with all kinds of social media notifications. When did they expect professionals such as himself to keep up with all of that? He scratched the budding signs of his newly forming beard and made a mental note to shave.

He wondered if anyone had responded to the subtle snooping Gabby had been doing on social media. They needed to find anyone who had dealings with the senator's daughter. He had nothing to lose by checking so he checked the bait account that Gabby had set up. Then he posted as many variations of the same set of questions, hoping to spark something in someone, anyone. Then he browsed as he waited.

Before he could stop himself, he put his head down on the desk and fell asleep. When he awoke, it was already ten o'clock. He checked the computer one last time before shutting it down for the night. There were three messages in his inbox and he rubbed his eyes as he read them , one by one. He couldn't believe what he was reading but he knew he had to talk to Gabby. He stumbled over to the phone, trying to reach her. It rang only once, then went directly to voicemail.

"Man," he said. He had forgotten that she couldn't receive calls at the shelter after ten o clock and her cell phone kept going to voice mail. It was late and there was nothing else he could do. Thankfully the hearing wasn't until 2:00pm the next afternoon and he had taken the day off from work. So he went to bed, planning to call Gabby early the next morning.

He tossed and turned all night, thinking about Caleb and the trial. When the first signs of morning entered the room, he leaped out of bed with anticipation. He couldn't wait for the stupid alarm clock. He grabbed his phone and began dialing, hoping that someone would answer the phone. After trying several times, he decided to give it a break before calling again.

He peeled off of his clothes and jumped into a nice warm shower, believing that it would give everyone enough time to wake up. After all, Home Again opened at eight o'clock every morning and it was already seven thirty.

When he came out of the bathroom he dressed in his white shirt and navy blue two piece suit for court because it would be a busy day and he certainly wasn't planning on coming back home to change. Then he tried to reach Home Again for the third time that morning. He let it ring numerous times, then hung up. As he straightened his tie in the mirror, he tried the number again.

Finally, Ms. Baptiste answered.

"Good morning. Home Again Women's Transitional Shelter, how may I assist you?"

He recognized her voice right away. "Morning, Ms. Baptiste, it's me Devin."

"Oh, hi Devin. How are you, son?"

Devin tapped his pencil on the desk, anxiously. "I'm good. But I was hoping I could speak to Gabby, please."

"I'm afraid not." Ms. Baptiste sighed. "I wish I could but Gabby never came home last night."

Devin put his pencil down. "Never came home?"

"Nope. That's not like her at all. We have a few who get in trouble for breaking curfew every now and then but never Gabby," she said.

Devin wasn't sure what to think. "I've got some very important information to give her for the hearing."

"Well, she's not here and I have no idea where she is."

"I'll be right over." Devin hung up the phone and as fast as he could slip into his finest black Italian leather shoes, he was gone.

When Devin pulled up in front of the shelter, he was grateful to find a parking space for his car. He hopped out, then after electronically locking the doors, took the front steps two at a time. To say that he was anxious was an understatement. He rang the bell, then opened the door as he was buzzed in by Mr. Williams.

"Morning, Mr. Williams."

Mr. Williams looked at him sideways. "Hello, Son. You're out mighty early, aren't you?"

Devin said, "Yes, sir. It's a big day and so I thought I'd get an early start."

"Are you here to see Ms. Baptiste? She's in the living room right now." Mr. Williams mumbled as he shook his head." There's a lot going on... a lot going on, Son."

Devin walked from the lobby through the hallway to the living room. He heard voices as he walked through the double doors.

"Good morning Ms. Baptiste."

Ms. Baptiste's face looked distraught. "Oh, Devin, you're here."

"What's wrong?"

She furrowed her eyebrows. "I just received a very disturbing call, not more than five minutes ago."

Devin's heart began beating faster. "What is it?"

"It's Gabby. She's been in some kind of accident and she's in the hospital," she said.

Devin stepped back, putting his hand up to his forehead in dismay. "Oh, no. How did that happen?"

"I don't have the details except that she's at Harlem Hospital and they say she's in critical condition."

"I've got to go," Devin said.

"Wait. Let me get my purse and I'll ride with you. Let me grab this paper with her parent's contact information on it so I can notify them on the way." Ms. Baptiste ripped out a piece of note paper.

"Wow, she actually gave you her parent's number?" Devin asked.

Ms. Baptiste took off her glasses. "No, but they slipped it to me at the street festival. I'll tell them to meet us at the hospital."

"Let's go," Devin said.

Devin and Ms. Baptiste ran out to the lobby.

Mr. Williams stood up. "Where are you two going in such a hurry?"

"Mr. Williams, I just received a phone call from Harlem Hospital and there has been an emergency with Gabby."

TWENTY-FOUR

I pushed through the double doors to the emergency room lobby and there they were. "What's going on here?" I said, bursting onto the scene.

Ms. Baptiste dropped her purse to the floor. "Gabby?"

Devin ran over to me. "Gabrielle, you're okay."

"Of course, I'm okay. Why does everybody look like you've seen a ghost?"

Ms. Baptiste put her hands over her mouth. "Oh, thank the Lord."

Devin started, "We thought you were…"

"Thought I was what?" I was so confused at this point.

Ms. Baptiste put her hand up to her forehead. "If you're not hurt…how did you know we were here?"

"Well, I went home and Mr. Williams told me to get down to Harlem Hospital Emergency room fast, that everybody was down here. He didn't bother to explain why so I came right over. What's going on?"

"We were told that you were here in critical condition," Ms. Baptiste said, almost out of breath.

This was nonsense. I pointed to myself. "Well, obviously I'm not."

"Thank God for that but," Ms. Baptiste said.

Devin shook his head. "I don't understand."

I looked around the room at everyone who was sitting down. "Neither do I. I mean who told you I was hurt and why are you all here? I mean…"

"Well, we're waiting for your parents," Ms. Baptiste explained.

I closed my eyes before speaking. "My parents. You're kidding me right?"

Ms. Baptiste held her head down. "No. I had to let them know you were dying."

"But I'm not … dying." I shook my head. "Why would you think that?"

Ms. Baptiste continued, "But the hospital called and said so and then you didn't come home so…"

I squinted my eyes as I struggled to understand. "Are you sure they said *my* name?"

Devin jumped in. "Yes, but when we came in, they told us that only the next of kin would be able to visit you. We were just sitting here waiting for your parents…"

Now my head was spinning. "Wow, I don't know what's going on but ..."

All of a sudden I remembered something. I put my hand up to cover my mouth. "Oh, my goodness."

Ms. Baptiste looked distraught. "What? What is it?"

I felt a knot in my stomach. "I think I know what happened."

Devin came closer to me. "What?"

I looked straight at Ms. Baptiste. "It's Ashley. It has to be Ashley in there. Did she come home last night?"

"No, actually she didn't come home either," Ms. Baptiste answered.

My heart began to beat fast. "She has my ID. Nothing with a picture on it or anything but she asked if she could borrow my library card."

Devin stood in front of me. "But why?"

"To make a long story short, about a week ago she wanted to check out a few books for a class assignment. She'd lost hers. Said she didn't have the time or patience to get another one right now. She didn't want to hear Ms. Baptiste's lecture about her losing her card in the first place. So she borrowed mine." I walked over to the nurses desk in a daze.

"Oh no. So it's Ashley in there?" Ms. Baptiste ran up to the front desk behind me. She explained about the mix up and asked for a description of the patient. Long blonde hair was the first thing they said and so it was confirmed. "Oh my goodness and your parents are on their way, Gabby."

"That's right, my parents." I didn't have time to ask how she was able to reach them. "Devin, may I borrow your phone? Mine is dead."

"Sure," he said.

I tried to call home but it was too late. There was no answer, even on their cells. *What could they be thinking?*

By the time we sat down Devin went to get us cups of coffee. He liked his black. I liked mine with cream and sugar. Ms. Baptiste liked only Splenda in hers.

About twenty minutes later my parents came running into the waiting area.

"Oh Gabby." Mom hugged me tighter than she ever had. "Thank God you're all right."

"I'm fine, Mom. I tried to call to tell you that there's been a big misunderstanding," I began to explain.

Dad hugged me next, then let out a sigh of relief. "But we were told that-"

"I know, I know and I'm sorry." I shook my head. "There's been a mix up-a mistaken identity of sorts."

"I'm sorry; that was my fault," Ms. Baptiste said. "It wasn't your daughter but her roommate, Ashley.

Dad asked, "Her roommate?"

"Yes." Ms. Baptiste nodded. "She had Gabby's library card on her. Mom looked confused. "But how?"

I jumped in. "She'd borrowed my library card and that's the ID they found on her. It had the shelter's name on it too and that's how they were able to call."

"I had all of the women mark their library cards with a Home Again sticker so if anything ever happened to any of them, we'd know. You'd be surprised at how many of the women don't have any other ID," Ms. Baptiste explained, solemnly.

"I see," Mom said.

"But I'm so glad it wasn't you." Dad straightened his face when he realized how uncaring he sounded. "I didn't mean it like that but I mean I'm sorry about your friend."

"We're all worried about her," I said. Looking at him reminded me of how Devin and I had to bring him home the other night. I was so done with him.

Mom looked genuinely concerned. "What's wrong with your roommate?"

I shrugged my shoulders. "We don't know any of the details yet."

Just then a doctor came out and proceeded to look at his chart. "We were told that there was some kind of mix up and that the young lady, Ashley Claremont has no next of kin so the shelter director is responsible for her," he said.

Ms. Baptiste stood up and walked over to him. "That would be me, Sir."

The doctor looked up from his chart. "Ashley has a severe concussion. We're trying to lessen the pressure around the brain from the swelling. Right now, we're concerned most about the hemorrhaging.

Ms. Baptiste asked. "May I ask what happened to her?"

The doctor looked around, then whispered. "Apparently, the poor girl walked in front of a moving vehicle. It appears that she was quite under the influence."

"Oh no," Ms. Baptiste said, hanging her head.

I closed my eyes and listened.

"Substance abuse is a very serious problem," the doctor said, pulling his pencil from behind his ear. He began to write something on the chart. "It looks like she may have collapsed in the street and it's actually a good thing she did because there was so much heroin in her system that if she hadn't gotten run over, she probably would've died hours ago from the overdose. She's lucky to be alive."

Ms. Baptiste grabbed the doctor's hand. "May I see her, please?"

"I don't think that would be a problem but just for a moment. It may be good for brain activity. So far she hasn't been responding," the doctor explained. "We're trying to determine whether or not she'll need surgery. Oh and if you can get in touch with any family of hers, that would be helpful." The doctor walked away, then looked back. "You should also request a chaplain. She may not make it through the night."

We all stood in silence as Ms. Baptiste followed the doctor in to see Ashley.

"I can't believe this." All of a sudden I heard loud sobs and wondered where they were coming from. I was even more shocked when I realized they were coming from my father.

I went over to my father and patted him on the back. "What's going on here?"

Mom looked as startled as I was. "I don't even know, sweetheart. I guess it's all just too much for him."

"No, that's not it at all." My father was shaking. "It's that girl…. Ashley."

I sat next to him. "What about her?"

My father began to speak slowly, in between sobs. "She's in there fighting for her life because she has a drug problem and maybe she hasn't dealt with it. Maybe if she had, none of us would be here right now. When the doctor said she probably won't make it through the night, my heart just went out to her. When we were driving over here we thought it was Gabrielle but now I realize that it's not her that's dying; it's that young girl and it's me."

"What are you talking about?" Mom asked.

"It's me, my life. That young girl is addicted to drugs-heroine I think the doctor said. But

I'm addicted too," Dad said.

I couldn't believe my ears. I looked at Devin and he looked at me but no one dared to say a single word.

"Gabrielle, I'm so sorry. Since the other night I've been so ashamed but then I tried to ignore it cause I've lived most of my adult life this way."

I tried to stop him from making a scene. "Dad, please…"

"And for years you've been trying to tell me, trying to show me, then Teshaun and Barry…" Dad paused. "We lost them but I didn't understand why you were so angry with me. But the drunk driver that killed your family, the one that's locked up right now, I am that person. I've driven drunk before. No matter how much I don't want to be , I'm that person."

"Don't," Mom said.

"No, I have to do this. I'm that addicted person and I've been tormented for years. I

should've listened long ago." Dad reached out to me and I fell into his arms. "Will you please forgive me? "

"Yes." I didn't know what else to say. "Of course."

Then Dad sat down in a seat, still sobbing, and bowed his balding head. "Sadie, will you help me to get some help?"

"I will," Mom sat next to him and began to rub his head.

We all had center stage as everyone in the waiting room listened to and whispered about our conversation. I didn't matter anymore what anyone thought anyway.

"Thank you, Jesus," I whispered.

Devin snapped his fingers. "Speaking of help, I almost forgot that I came over earlier to give you some information about Caleb's case. I hate to interrupt this family moment but uh…"

"Wow, in all of this excitement, I almost forgot about the hearing today," I said.

Devin pulled me to the side and began to whisper. "I tried to get with you last night but it was too late for you to receive calls and then this morning when Ms. Baptiste said you hadn't been home, I was very concerned." Devin studied for face, waiting for an explanation.

"I didn't know that my not coming home would matter to anybody except Ms. Baptiste." I looked away.

Devin gently turned my face back to face him. "Are you kidding me? You had me frantic this morning."

"I figured you'd be busy with your fiancé," I smirked.

Devin nodded. "Ex-fiancé. Is that what your disappearance was all about?"

"Well, I stopped by your apartment last night to talk about the case and to say I was sorry about giving you such a hard time but just as I turned the corner, I saw her going into your building."

"So you saw Dana?"

"Yes and I was reminded of how pretty she was and how much you cared about her so I figured that the three of you would be happy together. I'm never going to stand in the way of a family. So I just left," I explained

Devin smiled to himself. "But you never went back to the shelter?"

I fluttered my eyelashes. "No, I went to my friend Uma's apartment and spent the evening talking. I did leave a voicemail but I guess Ms. Baptiste never got a chance to listen to it this morning."

Devin stared into my eyes, making me nervous. "Why didn't you call me?"

I shrugged. "I had nothing to say. Besides, I didn't want to be a burden or anything. I mean you with your recently found son and everything…" I started to turn my body away but he held onto both arms like a desperate man.

Devin wouldn't let me go. "First of all, you're not a burden. I tried to call and apologize for how things went down the other day but you wouldn't accept my calls. And there's nothing between me and Dana; her son is not even mine."

 I looked into his warm eyes. "How can you be so sure?"

"Dana told me that she cheated with another man, a director she wanted to work with and that man is her son's father; she's sure about that," Devin said.

I felt terrible for him. "I'm sorry."

"Don't be. It was just a pipe dream." Devin pushed a single strand of hair from my face. "I'm probably too old to be a father now anyway."

"I don't agree with that. You're not too old for anything." I tried to contain my happiness. "What about the mother?"

Devin made his eyes wide. "What about her?"

I was afraid of the answer but I had to ask anyway. "Do you still care for her?"

"My feelings for her ended a long, long time ago. The only thing we had recently were memories and most of those weren't good," Devin said.

"I'm sorry." I watched his eyes dance with excitement.

"Stop being sorry. It was never meant to be. If you had returned my calls, I would've told you that last night." Devin wouldn't stop staring.

I glanced up at the wall clock. "None of that's important right now; look at the time."

Devin said, "We've still got enough time to get you to the shelter so you can change your clothes, then make it to the courthouse on time."

"Ok," I said. "Mom and Dad, I'm due in court soon so I'll have to call you later."

Mom looked over her glasses, skeptically. "Gabby...I..."

"No, really; I promise I'll call." I hugged them both and noticed that my father was still drying his tears when I left. "Dad, it looks like you're in good hands- God's hands."

Mom smiled through her own tears.

As we drove to our destination, Devin filled me in on the updated social media messages. Thankfully, I was able to make some last minute phone calls, including one to a Kelly Bryant. Devin pulled up in front of the family court building and let me out. Then he proceeded to go find parking. I ran inside, scoped the lobby, then decided on the ladies room. My nerves were working on me and I was worried about perspiring underneath my arms. I needed to freshen up. I did a little dance inside the stall before I was able to relieve myself. As soon as my door swung open, I was face to face with Alexis Harvey.

"Well, well, well, what do you know, we meet again, Ms. Gabrielle McBay," Alexis smirked.

"Alexis." I washed my hands and refused to do more than acknowledge her.

Alexis walked right up to me. "Nice suit." She touched my arm.

"Thanks." I adjusted my skirt without even looking at her.

"Well, I see you've got a nice outfit and a leather briefcase. But are you ready to tango with me, darling?"

Now she had my attention and I looked into her hate filled eyes. "All day long...bring it."

Alexis giggled, then took a step back. "Very confident words for a bag lady. Yes, I know about your little stint at the Home Again Women's Transitional Shelter. I'm surprised you were able to tear yourself away from your little indigent friends. Oh and don't you have a curfew?"

I began to get hot. "At least some of my shelter friends have more integrity in their pinky fingers than you have in your whole body."

"Boo hoo." Alexis pretended to rub her eyes. "Poor little Gabrielle, lost her marbles and now she's back to collect them."

I clapped my hands. "Are you finished with your speech? Are you feeling better about yourself now? Do you feel really big for trying to make others seem small?"

Alexis pointed her finger towards me. "You don't know who you're messing with. You'd better be ready for me, sister, because unlike you. I'm not just playing with the law. And as far as protecting that little thug in there, we'll see about that." Alexis turned on her heels and left the restroom. "May the best attorney win."

TWENTY-FIVE

Family court was always busy, with cases being resolved at all times of the day. This day was obviously no different as attorneys, judges, caseworkers, probation officers, and parents all waited for their cases to be heard. Whether they were there for juvenile delinquent, custody, or child support hearings, we were all in the same tense situation—preparing, then waiting.

I yawned as I walked into the lobby.

Devin asked, "Are you bored or tired?"

"Are you kidding me? I'm never bored when I'm at the courthouse. Just a little tired. I didn't get much sleep last night, remember?"

"I couldn't sleep either." Devin stared at me. "But you look great."

I felt awkward as Devin's eyes scanned me so I decided to ignore his comment. "I can't believe it has been a whole thirty days."

"Me either. The month just flew by," Devin agreed, taking his eyes off me.

I pointed ahead of us. "Look, there's Caleb and his mom."

Devin walked towards them and grabbed Caleb. "I'm glad you all are here."

We exchanged polite words with Caleb and his mother before getting down to business.

I pulled Caleb close to me and whispered. "In this hearing we will discuss what physical evidence was found at the scene. From this the judge will determine whether or not you committed the acts charged in the petition. He'll also want to check on your progress since you've been on probation. So be on your best behavior."

Caleb's mother straightened Caleb's tie.

Caleb gently pulled away from her. "Progress?"

"He'll want to hear whether or not you've been attending school and staying out of trouble," I explained.

"That ain't nothing new," Caleb said.

"Anything. That isn't anything new. No, it's not but it'll be new to the judge," I continued.

Devin patted Caleb on the back.

Caleb looked nervous. "What if I'm found guilty?"

I gave him an *I'm sorry* look. "Well, in that case, the judge will schedule a dispositional hearing for about six weeks later. That's when he'll decide on your punishment-"

Caleb sighed. "My punishment for something I didn't do?"

Devin and I looked at each other.

"Well, the judge can still dismiss the case even at the dispositional hearing if he feels that supervision, treatment or confinement would not help. He can also grant an adjournment in contemplation for dismissal."

Ms. Johnson asked, "What's that?"

"It's kind of like an extension and the judge can grant it for up to six months. Or he can issue a conditional discharge. Or in some cases he can give probation for up to two years."

Caleb dropped his head.

Devin interrupted, "But we're holding out for the case to be dropped, right Gabby?"

I glanced at Devin before turning back to Caleb and his mother. "Yes, of course, we're hoping to get your case dismissed completely. If we can poke enough holes in Victoria's story, we can get exactly that. Now here is what Devin found last night."

Caleb and his mother looked at Devin.

Devin handed them a sheet of paper. "I found a witness and it's last minute so we don't know how credible she is, but we're going for it."

"Go for it." Caleb nodded.

Devin put his fist in the air. "With God on our side, nothing is impossible."

I looked around to see who noticed. A warm feeling flooded me inside. "Right, nothing is impossible."

A small crowd had started to gather, but not the media; I'd made sure of that. Even the senator had to play by the rules in court. Devin led us away from the hustle and bustle. There were chairs lining the wall outside our hearing room so we sat in them. Devin bowed his head and I knew he was praying. Something inside me made me want to pray too. I grabbed Caleb's hand and then Devin's. Devin looked up at me, then whispered a soft prayer aloud. His words seemed to stir something in me I couldn't control.

Just then the court officer came out and called us into the room. Devin nodded and we all dispersed.

It had been a long time since I'd been in family court. I took Caleb to sit with me. Ms. Johnson sat next to Devin. Alexis sat on the opposite side of the room, with her legs crossed. She was busy arranging her papers in front of her. Senator Dawson, his impeccably dressed wife, and his daughter walked in together. They sat a couple of rows behind Alexis. Victoria was dressed in a conservative white dress. *Good choice.*

I noticed the court reporter, perched in her place, ready to type the transcript at the start of the hearing. The court clerk sat near the judge, waiting. I also noticed a probation officer, ready to investigate and prepare his report for the judge. Seconds later, the judge entered, wearing his regal black robe, and sat at his bench in the front of the room. He was a stocky, middle aged man who was so pale I wondered if he ever went out into the sun. Surprisingly, I didn't recognize him so I considered the fact that he might be new to the bench. His court clerk bent down and whispered to him. The United States flag stood in the background. Although I was a little shaky, I couldn't wait to get back into the fight. I missed the courtroom antics.

Alexis kept looking over at me and Caleb as if she was expecting me to give up and run away any minute. Once our eyes met and she rolled hers.

The court clerk introduced the honorable, Judge Callahan. Then we were instructed to give our opening addresses. I cringed the whole time Alexis gave hers.

"Your honor, members of the jury, I am Alexis Harvey, the prosecuting attorney and I represent the state. I will prove its case through witnesses and other evidence the allegations of the delinquency petition beyond a reasonable doubt. In order to prove grand theft auto, I will prove that the defendant, Caleb Johnson, drove the vehicle that it belonged to someone else, Senator Dawson. The intent was to permanently deprive the owner of his vehicle in a twisted attempt to get back at the senator for him not allowing him to date his daughter."

Then it was my turn to set the tone for our case.

I am Gabrielle McBay and I represent the respondent, Caleb Johnson. I will confront and cross examine all witnesses and present tangible evidence to prove that Caleb Johnson could not have committed this crime. My client has been charged with grand theft auto and it is my intention to prove that my client did not steal the car in question but merely became a pawn in a complicated game Victoria Dawson decided to play. My client is an honor student and scholarship applicant who up until the time he was detained in custody, had perfect school attendance. He also has absolutely no prior offences on his record. He never intended to keep the senator's car or to steal the senator's car but to merely borrow it with the permission of the owner's daughter. Instead, he was merely a pawn in a selfish game. We will show that the prosecution's witnesses' credibility is poor as well. We will ultimately show that the defendant is not guilty of grand theft auto but that this is a game of love and politics gone wrong, your honor."

"Your honor, this is no game. This is just a case of a wreck less child gone bad. I would like to present my first witness, Senator Dawson."

I watched Senator Dawson tighten his tie as he approached the witness stand. After being sworn in, Alexis started her theatrics.

"Senator Dawson, where were you on May 28th 2022? At approximately midnight?"

"I received a call from the local police department that they had found my car with a teenager driving it. I was actually surprised they'd found it so fast because I'd just reported it stolen not that long before."

"Did they tell you who stole your car, Mr. Dawson?"

"Yes, they did eventually but that wasn't until I went down to the station. I was shocked to find out that it was Caleb after all I'd done for him but It all made sense."

Alexis continued, "What exactly made sense Senator?"

"Well, Caleb had the access to my office since he'd been working with me for a few days and he knew where I kept my spare key. I'm sure my Range Rover was very alluring for a boy his age."

Alexis asked, "Sir, you almost sound sympathetic towards him and what he's done?"

"Not at all. I was all for giving him a chance to prove himself to be a good citizen but now that he has turned around and done such a thing, I want him prosecuted to the fullest extent of the law. I am tough on crime in this city, even when it's done by juvenile delinquents."

"How did you discover that your Range Rover was stolen?"

"Well, I was on my way to a business trip out of the country but my ride was late picking me up and we got stuck in traffic before getting to the airport." The senator stopped to clear his throat. "To make a long story short, I missed my flight, or at least I missed the cut off time to board the plane. They told me I could catch the next flight early the next morning."

"I see." Alexis peered at the senator with a fake smile on her face the whole time.

"So when I was dropped off at the office to pick up my vehicle, it was gone. The first thing I did was to call my wife, of course, to ask if she'd taken it and she said that she hadn't. So that's when I reported it stolen. I had no idea it would come to this with this criminal, Caleb Johnson."

"Objection." I stood up and shouted. "Caleb has not yet been found guilty."

"Objection sustained," the judge said. "Be careful how you refer to the respondent."

"Sorry, your honor," Senator Dawson said.

Alexis bowed slightly. "Thank you, Sir. No more questions."

Then Judge Callahan asked if I wanted to cross examine her witness and you bet I did. The senator looked so phony sitting up there as if he was playing a role for all of his constituents. I was disgusted. *Be real, my brother.*

"Senator Dawson, you said that you were surprised to learn that Caleb was the one driving your car, correct?"

Senator Dawson nodded at me. "Yes, that's correct."

I opened my arms wide. "Did it ever cross your mind, once you found out the identity of the driver, that perhaps there was a logical explanation? Did you ever give Caleb Johnson the benefit of the doubt?"

Senator Dawson didn't blink. "No, there was really no need because I never gave him or anyone else permission to drive my Range Rover."

I took a deep breath because he was a tough one. "Fair enough. Do you have an office at home, Senator?"

Senator Dawson coughed. "Of course, I do."

"And does it stay locked most of the time when you're away?"

"Yes, it does."

"But if you were to come home one day and find that your daughter had been in your office, sat in your chair, touched your desk, even without your permission, would you be upset?"

Senator Dawson sighed. "No, but that's not the same thing."

"Just a moment, please." I put up my hand to indicate a pause." But your office is generally off limits to your daughter isn't it?"

"Yes," the senator huffed.

I continued, "And so is the Range Rover off limits?"

Senator Dawson was smooth. "That's right."

"But your daughter does have a driver's license doesn't she?"

"Of course she does."

"So it is possible that she could actually drive the Range Rover just like it is possible that she could come into your office and sit at your desk."

"I suppose so," he admitted, hesitantly.

"So did you ever consider the fact that your teenage daughter, having communication with Caleb Johnson, could have been a part of the decision to take your vehicle from its parking spot?"

"My daughter does not communicate with Caleb Johnson and no she did not have anything to do with it," Senator Dawson said.

I tried to face the audience so I could see their reaction. "Oh, I believe that she does. And why then, in your opinion, would a studious young man like Caleb Johnson, risk his reputation and his academic career which he has worked so hard for to steal your vehicle?"

"I don't know, for money maybe. Or for revenge," the senator said.

I tiptoed over to the witness stand. "Revenge for what, Sir, may I ask?"

"Well, he wanted to date my daughter and I forbade that. I'm a very strict parent, you know."

I went right up to his face. "Are you? How did you feel about Caleb? Did you think he wasn't good enough for your daughter?"

The senator's face looked cold and blank. "It was nothing like that."

"Well, what was it, Senator? Surely, if he was good enough to give a speech at your fundraising dinner and receive a standing ovation I might add, and work in your office, then surely this young man must be an upstanding citizen. You made a public comment about how pleased you were about him. Did you not mean that?"

Senator Dawson's face remained hardened. "You are twisting my words around. I never said that he wasn't an upstanding citizen…"

"Really? When this trial started you said you were surprised to find out he was a criminal. Which is it? Is he a good citizen or a criminal? And why would an upstanding citizen steal your car, Senator ?"

"I meant that I thought he was a good kid until he stole my Range Rover," Senator Dawson explained.

I made my voice go up an octave which I was sure was irritating. "But we haven't proven yet that he stole your car, just that he was driving it. He has made statements to the police that your daughter was riding in the vehicle with him."

"That's impossible." Senator Dawson frowned.

I knew I was treading on thin ice but I went there anyway. "Can you prove that she wasn't in the vehicle?"

Alexis jumped up and held up one finger. "Objection, your honor. It is not the witnesses' responsibility to prove anything."

"Objection sustained. Get on with it, McBay," The judge snapped.

"I'm sorry, your honor." I smiled at the judge, then at Alexis. "No further questions."

I'd hoped that I succeeded in planting doubt in the judge's mind. Only time would tell.

Alexis gave me a dirty look. She called her next witness , Victoria Dawson, and I could hardly wait to tear her testimony apart. Victoria climbed up to the witness stand, identified herself and was sworn in. She tossed her long, straight hair about her shoulders.

Alexis looked confident in her two piece designer suit. "Victoria, where were you on April 28th 2022 at 12:00 midnight?"

Victoria paused. "I was at my friend Sandra's house. I slept over and by midnight we were already asleep."

Alexis twiddled her thumbs. "So you never went out on a date with Caleb Johnson on that night?"

"No. Not at all. He asked if we could go out sometimes but my dad was against it." She pressed her thin lips together.

Alexis turned her back to Victoria for a moment. "I'll bet he was. And when you told Caleb Johnson no, how did he feel about it?"

"He felt angry," Victoria whispered.

I interrupted, "Objection. This is hearsay. The prosecution is asking the witness to speculate about my client's feelings."

"Objection sustained," the judge said.

Alexis walked back and forth across the front. "All right then. What did Caleb Johnson say when you turned him down?"

Victoria shrugged her shoulders. "He said he was upset."

Alexis probed. "Is that all?"

Victoria looked down at her hands. "Yeah, that's all. He didn't really want to talk anymore."

Alexis stood still in front of Victoria. "So he was so angry that he didn't even want to talk to you anymore?"

I stood up. "Objection, your honor. Again this is all speculation. No facts."

"Objection sustained. Stick to the facts here, Ms. Harvey." Judge Callahan said.

"Sorry, your honor. That will be all," Alexis said.

I could see her snide expression from my peripheral vision. It was my turn to approach the bench. Without hesitation, I went in on her. "Victoria. First of all you testified that you spent the night with your friend Sandra and that you all went to bed early. Isn't that a little unusual for two teenage girls on a sleepover?"

Victoria shifted her position in the seat. "We uh were tired after watching the movies."

"They must've been some kind of movies. What did you see?"

"Just some random stuff on Netflix," she said.

I looked at the audience quizzically. "So you don't even remember what you saw? "

"Not really," Victoria said.

"That must've been some boring sleepover," I added.

The audience chuckled a bit and whispered. Immediately, I began to feed off of their energy.

Victoria shrugged her shoulders but didn't respond.

"When you met Caleb at your father's fundraising dinner, did you like him?"

Victoria batted her eyelashes but I was unimpressed. "He was okay."

"Just okay? But we have several witnesses who signed statements saying that you were all over him at that event." I held up the signed statements. "We even have pictures. They're all over Instagram."

The judge asked, "May I see those?"

I handed him the papers and continued, "So like I said people talk and most people saw you in Caleb Johnson's face looking very interested in him."

"Objection." Alexis said through almost clenched teeth. "She's badgering my witness."

The judge looked over his glasses. "Where are you going with this, Ms. McBay?"

"Your honor, I'm trying to establish the fact that there was some leading on that night in order to establish the basis for this relationship," I explained.

"Objection overruled; I'll allow it," the judge said.

I looked Victoria in the eyes. "Thank you. Now would you answer my question, please?"

Victoria swallowed hard. "Would you please repeat the question?"

I started again, "Sure. Did you act like you liked Caleb Johnson on the night of your father's dinner?"

"No... I mean maybe. I don't know," Victoria snapped.

"Humph, touchy subject I guess." I looked over at Alexis and smiled. "You don't know? How could you not know if you liked him or not? Witnesses say you kept talking to him and you went to the back of the room with him. You appeared to be giggling. Those are facts."

"He kept talking to me and I... we just kept talking," Victoria spat out.

I clenched my hands together in front of my mouth. "So you did like Caleb then, at least enough to talk to him off and on all night? And you must have thought he was funny if you were giggling, right?"

Victoria started playing with her fingers on the stand. "Yeah, I mean he was cool, I guess."

"You guess? You're a big girl, seventeen years old and intelligent. I'm sure you're able to articulate to me or anyone else how you really felt about Caleb Johnson. After all, you had your father and security and a whole crowd of people to back you up; if Caleb Johnson was really bothering you and you didn't like him, couldn't you have just ignored him?"

"I didn't want to be rude," Victoria said, quietly.

"Of course not. But Caleb says it was more than that. He says you pretended to like him and he also says you were together on the night in question even though you weren't supposed to be. Is that true?"

Victoria shook her head vigorously. "No, I was at home with my friend, Sandra."

I ignored her answer. "But even if you wanted to be with Caleb, your father would not approve is that correct?"

"Yes."

I came up close to her. "Because he felt Caleb was not good enough for his daughter, is that correct?"

Alexis stood up. "Objection. This is getting ridiculous."

"Objection sustained," the judge said. "Lead us out of here, Ms. McBay."

"Yes, your honor." I took a deep breath. "So is it possible that you went over to your friend's house so you could go out with Caleb, without your father's knowledge, because you knew he wouldn't approve?"

"No," Victoria answered quickly.

I walked, then stopped in front of Victoria. "Did anyone besides your friend, Sandra, see you after ten o' clock pm? Maybe her parents?"

Victoria's eyebrows began to meet in the middle. "No, Sandra and I went upstairs early to watch movies and stuff."

I studied her face for changes in expression. "Were you aware that your father's Range Rover was stolen?"

"Not until the next day when he told me." Victoria looked down.

Finally, it was time. I held up the photograph. "Do you know a guy by the name of Zack T?"

TWENTY-SIX

It was just beginning to get good. I stared out into the audience for a moment. I noticed Senator Dawson whispering to his wife. Caleb nervously thumped his fingers on the desk in front of him. Then I turned on my heels and glanced at the wall clock. Time was ticking away. When I looked up at the judge, even he was sitting on the edge of his seat.

"Yeah, I know of him." Victoria squirmed in her seat.

I nodded. "Would you please describe the nature of your relationship?"

"He's just some dude I met through a friend." Victoria looked agitated.

I asked, "He doesn't attend your school?"

"No," she said.

I came right up to her. "So are you two dating?"

"Objection, your honor." Alexis stood up, fuming.

"This information is irrelevant."

I was ready for this. "On the contrary, your honor, this information is very relevant. I'm trying to establish relationships with this gentleman so as to verify her whereabouts on the night in question."

The judge frowned at me. "Again, I'll allow it. Get to the point, Ms. McBay."

"Yes, your honor." I turned from the judge to face the witness stand. "Victoria, are you dating or have you ever dated Zack Thompson, known as Zack T?"

Victoria continued to fidget in her seat. "Well, he liked me once but…"

I interrupted, "But your father wouldn't allow it either…"

Alexis jumped up. "Objection. Badgering the witness."

The Judge used her gavel. "Objection sustained."

"Fine, no further questions, your honor." I went to sit down.

When I went back to my seat, Caleb passed me bottled water. I drank it down in two or three gulps and hoped my bladder could hold up afterwards.

I watched Victoria Dawson leave the witness stand and sit next to her father. She avoided looking at Caleb or me.

Alexis came forward. "I would like to call Sandra McMillan to the stand."

Sandra, a tall teenager with light green eyes and dark brown hair climbed up to the witness stand, identified herself and was sworn in.

Alexis angled herself in front of the judge. "Sandra, did Victoria Dawson spend the night at your house on May 28th 2022?"

"Yes, she did." Sandra looked into the audience at Victoria. "And we had a lot of fun."

Alexis bounced around the judge's desk like she owned it. "You two had a lot of fun because you're best friends, correct?"

Sandra smiled. "Yes, we are."

Alexis stopped in front of Alexis. "And did your parents see Victoria that evening?"

Sandra nodded as if she was cued. "Yes, they saw her as soon as she came over which was about seven o' clock."

"And what did the two of you do while she was there?"

Sandra spoke slowly. "We watched movies and talked, painted our fingernails…"

Alexis smiled at the girl. "Typical girl sleepover stuff, huh?"

"Yep."

Alexis faced the audience. "Did Caleb Johnson come over to your house?"

"No way," Sandra said.

Alexis spun around on her heels. "And did Victoria leave your house at any time for any reason on that night?"

Sandra made a face. "No, why would she do that? We were having a girl's night."

"Yes, that's exactly what it sounds like." Alexis walked back to her seat. "No further questions, your honor."

I walked by Alexis and came up to Sandra McMillan like I was on a mission. "Sandra, did your parents see Victoria at any time after ten o'clock pm?"

"Uh after ten?

"Yes, after ten."

"Probably not because we'd gone upstairs by then and they'd gone to bed too."

I had to make the judge doubt her innocence. "So you and your best friend were at home watching movies and painting toenails and probably talking about boys a little, am I correct?"

"Yeah... I guess," Sandra said.

"Was Caleb Johnson or Zack T one of those boys you were talking about?"

"Objection." Alexis sighed. "You are so out of line that this is embarrassing."

"Objection sustained." The judge warned, "McBay stick to the topic."

"I'm sorry, your honor." I took a deep breath. "Isn't it true that Victoria Dawson did in fact leave your house after ten o' clock to meet up with Caleb Johnson?"

"No, she was with me the whole time." Sandra's face was expressionless.

I came up close to her. "And isn't it true that not only did she meet up with Caleb but when the cops pulled him over in her father's car, she had a change in plans and Zack T met her and brought her back to your house?"

Sandra began to stutter. "No… she she never left."

I've struck a nerve. "Are you sure because you are in a court of law?"

Sandra looked like she had seen a ghost. "Yes, I'm sure."

I looked around the room casually. "Isn't it true that you and Victoria have been known to sneak out of the house to do other things, prohibited things?"

Sandra looked like she wanted to run off the stand. "Well, I…"

I stood in front of her and tapped my foot. "Isn't it true that you two were just caught a few months prior for sneaking out from another friend's house to go to a rap concert you were all banned from attending?"

Sandra began to sweat. "Yes, but…."

I continued, "So you two were used to sneaking out and covering for each other?"

"No… I mean yes but not that night. We stayed home that night," Sandra said, with a cracking voice.

"What makes that night any different than any other night? Did you take a no lying vow for that night?"

"Objection," Alexis huffed.

"Your honor, please. I'm trying to get there," I said.

"Get there, McBay," the judge threatened.

I had to trap her. "So you and your friend have snuck out of the house in the past without the parents of the house knowing about it, correct?"

When I saw Devin and Ms. Johnson gasp with anticipation, I knew that it was finally getting interesting. It was all coming back to me.

Sandra hung her head. "Yes."

"No further questions, your honor." I smiled in Devin's direction, hoping he knew I was smiling at him.

When it was my turn to call my witnesses, I called his name first.

Devin walked up to the front, identified himself and got sworn in. He looked so handsome sitting there on the witness stand, the way the light shone on his squared jaw, the way his suit jacket fit against his broad chest.

I started in on him right away. "Mr. Ramos or Mr. "D" as your students like to call you, what is your relationship to Caleb?"

Devin spoke, using his hands for emphasis. "I am his science teacher and I'd like to think that I'm a mentor of some sort."

I walked back and forth in front of the judge's desk. "And why would you call yourself that?"

Devin tried to explain so that the judge could understand. "Because with their parent's permission, every year I get very involved in the lives of a few select students and I like to make a mark in their lives, the same way someone once made a mark on mine."

I stopped in front of the witness stand and peered at Devin. "And what kind of student is Caleb Johnson?"

"He's a very bright kid, an A student with an even brighter future. In fact, he's a good candidate for a science scholarship he has already applied for." Devin looked out at Caleb as he spoke. "He's always respectful, helpful, and up until this incident he had perfect attendance."

For dramatic effect, I stretched my arms out wide. "So you've never had any problems with Caleb in your class?"

Devin continued, "Nope. Never. And as far as I know I don't think any other teacher has either."

"Objection. That's hear say," Alexis said.

The judge leaned forward. "Sustained. Stick to the facts, Mr. Ramos."

"Sorry, your honor," Devin said.

I continued, "When you saw Caleb after the Senator's fundraiser banquet, what did he say?"

Devin took his time to explain. "Well, he was so excited after the banquet that he had his mother drop him by my apartment that night for a few minutes. He told me that he'd had a great time, that he was proud of himself for the speech he gave. And he also told me that he met the senator's daughter."

"And what did he say about her?"

"He said that he liked her and that they were planning to go out," Devin said.

I had to break the prosecution's theory that he was vengeful. "Did he seem at all angry to you during this time?"

"No, actually he said she was very pretty and he seemed happy." Devin chuckled.

"Thank you, Mr. Ramos." I turned away from him. "No further questions, your honor."

I tiptoed back to my seat and gave Caleb a high five under the table.

Alexis forfeited her opportunity to cross examine him. I figured she knew to leave well enough alone. There was absolutely nothing in Caleb's records that could be held against him-nothing. And I was pretty sure she'd already checked.

Nervously, I looked around the courtroom for my secret weapon until I saw her sitting in the back of the room. She was smaller than most teenagers and her petite frame was over shadowed by a long flowery dress.

I was just getting into my stride. "Your honor, I would like to call my last witness, Kelly Bryant."

Kelly walked slowly up the aisle and settled in at the witness stand. She pushed a strand of her bright red hair from her freckled face. Kelly identified herself and was sworn in.

Everything was riding on this girl's testimony. I winked at Caleb. "Kelly, will you please explain your relationship to Caleb Johnson."

"None. I don't know him at all," Kelly said.

"But take a good look at him." I pointed to Caleb sitting in the front row." Have you ever seen him anywhere before today?"

Kelly shook her head. "No, I haven't."

I stepped in front on Kelly and grinned. "Would you please describe your relationship to Victoria Dawson?"

Kelly answered matter of factly, "She's just a girl I know from school. We've been in a few classes together over the years."

I leaned forward. "So you're classmates? Are you friends?"

"No, not really. I mean we're not enemies or anything." Kelly smiled softly. "We just don't hang out with the same people."

"But you certainly would've recognized her if you saw her?" I asked.

Kelly looked out into the audience. "Of course. We've known each other since junior high school."

I stepped aside. "Would you please point her out in the courtroom."

Kelly pointed straight ahead at Victoria.

"Yes, that's her." I held up a photograph. "Take a look at this photograph and tell me if you recognize this person."

Kelly studied the picture. "That's Zack T."

I eyed Kelly carefully. "And do you know him?"

"I know about him." Kelly pointed to the picture. "He's notorious for hitting on girls at our school."

I put the picture down. "Does he attend your school?"

"Oh no. Definitely not." Kelly shook her head. "I don't even think he goes to school anymore because I always see him hanging around outside all times of the day. I know he's been in trouble before."

I continued, "Have you ever seen this person, Zack T with Victoria Dawson?"

"Well, like I said, I've seen him talking to a lot of girls outside of school. But the only time I ever saw Zack T with Victoria was on the night of April 28th."

I put up two fingers. "So you saw the two of them together on April 28th at what time?"

"It was a little after midnight. It was a Friday and I was coming home from my cousin's birthday party. A male cousin was walking me home when I saw Victoria walking to Zack T's beat up Dodge Charger. He'd popped his head out the window and was yelling at her to hurry up." Kelly paused. "I was surprised to see her but I don't think she saw me. I told my cousin that she went to my school."

I asked, "What happened next?"

Kelly used her hands to demonstrate their actions. "She got in and Zack T pulled away in his car. It was kind of noisy. And that was the end of it."

I looked at the wall clock at the front of the room. "And you're sure about the time being a little after midnight?"

"Yep, because my uncle shut the party down at eleven thirty." Kelly looked at her watch. "It took my cousin thirty minutes just to get himself ready to walk me home. I don't live too far away but my uncle insisted."

"Of course. Thank you, Kelly." I walked back to my seat. "No further questions, your honor.

Alexis came up to cross examine. "Kelly, are you sure that you saw Victoria Dawson on the night in question?"

"Yes, I'm sure," Kelly said.

Alexis pointed to her face. "But you wear glasses. Are you sure you were wearing them on that night?"

"I always wear them; my eyesight is very bad." Kelly pushed her glasses up on her nose. "If I didn't wear them I'd be like whoa-blind."

"You said that you'd just left your cousin's party. Perhaps you weren't thinking clearly. Is it possible that you just thought you saw Victoria, when in fact, you actually saw someone *who looks* like Victoria? Is it possible that Zack T could've been with *someone else* who looks like Victoria?"

Kelly sighed. "Well, I guess anything is possible but I know what I saw."

Alexis asked, "Wouldn't it have been dark at midnight?"

"It would've been if it wasn't right there by the gas station. It's very well-lit there with all the stores."

Alexis turned her back to Kelly. "No further questions, your honor." I leaned over to whisper to Caleb. I didn't want him to testify but I had to make a last minute decision.

I decided to let the defense rest. I had given it my all and I was done.

Alexis rolled her eyes at me before starting her closing argument. "Good afternoon Your Honor, again my name is Alexis Harvey, and I am the prosecutor in this case. In my opening statement, I mentioned that I would call two witnesses to testify as to the defendant's guilt. Each witness testified and explained and we have established the following facts beyond a reasonable doubt: 1-that on May 28th, the defendant did intentionally take and drive Senator Dawson's Range Rover,2-Senator Dawson never gave Caleb permission to drive his Range Rover ,3-Caleb Johnson was out for revenge because he could not date the senator's daughter. We would ask you to reject the defense theory of the case. They would lead us to believe that this incident was just one big misunderstanding, that Caleb Johnson is an innocent victim. But we have proven here today that Senator Dawson is the true victim. After he has tried so hard to help the youth in the community, he allowed this boy to work in his office with his staff and Caleb Johnson took advantage of his kindness. In fact, he took the senator's kindness for weakness, and when Senator Dawson would not let his daughter date him, Caleb Johnson went out for revenge in the only way he knew how, by stealing the brand new car he knew the senator loved."

Her speech seemed to go on forever but when it was my turn, I rose to the occasion. *Lord, help me.* I walked out to the front with confidence.

"Good afternoon Your Honor, my name is Gabrielle McBay, and again I am the defense attorney in this case. In the case that the prosecutor presented to you there is insufficient evidence to convict my client. We would therefore ask for a verdict of not guilty. Yes, my client was caught driving the senator's car on the night in question because he had pseudo permission from the senator's daughter. She knew her father had left for his business trip and she coaxed Caleb to drive her around in it. Why? Because she had other plans. Caleb turned out just to be a pawn in the grand scheme of things. Victoria Dawson had already gotten herself mixed up with a bad boy but that boy was not Caleb. That's why she disappeared that night and pretended not to be with Caleb. When the police pulled him over, her plan had been ruined. Her real boyfriend was supposed to get that car and Caleb just got stuck in the middle. Sure her girlfriend said she was at her house all night. But that was just another act of teenage deception as they have admittedly engaged in before. And we have an eyewitness who finally had the courage to come forward and say that she saw Victoria Dawson in another car with another guy, a notorious gang banger, on the same night in question. How did that happen?"

"Does Victoria Dawson have a twin? How could she have been spotted with another guy on the same night? Is Victoria Dawson that popular that she would leave one boyfriend and go with another? Besides wasn't she supposed to be tucked in at the house of Sandra McMillan at a sleepover for the whole night? No she was not. Victoria Dawson was out with Caleb that night but not because she liked him; she wanted to use him so that her real boyfriend who has a rap sheet this long, including stealing cars, could get his greedy little hands on that Range Rover. And poor love sick Caleb would have to take the fall for it. He just got caught in the middle. So when her boyfriend saw that Caleb was being pulled over by the police, he was able to pick her up and take her back to her friend's house as quickly as his rimmed wheels could carry them? Now was Senator Dawson a victim? Maybe. Or maybe he wanted so badly to believe that his daughter was innocent that he refused to open his eyes and see that Caleb Johnson did not really steal his car or mean him any harm."

"We, the defense do not have to prove Caleb is innocent; instead, it is the burden of the prosecuting attorney to prove that the defendant is guilty without a shadow of doubt. Sadly, they have not met that burden. We would ask you to render the only verdict that is fair, not guilty."

TWENTY-SEVEN

When the judge announced the verdict of not guilty, I heard the words reverberate in my brain and in my spirit. The judge made a quick speech and wished Caleb well. I grabbed Caleb who was standing beside me and hugged him. "Halleluiah! We did it." Then, without even thinking, I leaped into Devin's arms and held on until I began to feel awkward about it. Then I peeled myself away. "Sorry," I said, dusting off his suit I'd wrinkled.

Devin looked confused. "Sorry for what?"

"I guess I got carried away.".

"It felt good." Devin smiled at me.

I could feel myself blushing. There were cheers, chatter, and conversations all around us yet at that moment it seemed as if we were the only two people in the room. After a moment, I snapped out of it and went over to hug Caleb's mother. "You've got your son back, Ms. Johnson."

Ms. Johnson threw her thick arms around me. "How can we ever thank you?"

"Don't thank me yet," I said with a straight face. "Wait until you see my bill."

Ms. Johnson looked startled and turned to look at Caleb..

I started to giggle and gave Caleb a fake punch. "Just kidding."

Ms. Johnson chuckled. Devin and Caleb laughed too.

It was such a wonderful accomplishment. I felt totally renewed.

Alexis came up to me while we were celebrating. "Don't think this is over, McBay. We'll meet again."

I looked her in the eyes and said. "We most certainly will." *I'll make your enemies your footstool.*

Then out of the crowd, Uma came up to me. "I'm so proud of you, Gabby. I knew you had in you."

"Thanks for being such a good friend to me at a time when I was so unfriendly and unreasonable."

"Don't mention it. I'm just glad that God is showing you how to climb out of the ashes."

"Yes, He is isn't He?" Then Devin, Caleb and I started jumping for joy until my legs and arms were tired and I was out of breath.

"Now let's all move forward, "Devin said, holding the three of us in a group hug.

"Let's start moving forward starting with this." Gabrielle reached into her pocket and pulled out a shiny object. "I guess I won't need this anymore.

Caleb furrowed his eyebrows. "What is that?"

She placed it around Caleb's neck. "It was one of my son's basketball medallions. I've been keeping it close for comfort for the past two years. But I want you to have it."

Caleb said, "Thanks."

Ms. Johnson smiled and nodded. Devin nodded in agreement.

The press followed us to the door. A reporter asked, "How do you feel about today's victory after not practicing law for so long?"

"All I have to say is all glory goes to God." And Devin helped us to push our way through the crowd.

Once we left the courthouse, Caleb, his mom, and a few of his relatives who had attended the trial, went out to celebrate.

Although we were exhausted, Devin and I went to visit Ashley. She was still in a coma but I spoke to her and Devin prayed for her before we left. It looked like she moved her eyelids while we were there but I couldn't be sure. And I didn't dare second guess God. I'd done way too much of that already. Ms. Baptiste met us at the hospital.

"I'm so proud of both of you," Ms. Baptiste said, hugging Devin and I.

Ernestine was there too, looking me up and down. She walked right up to me, put her hands up, and I braced myself for the worst; then I felt her arms settling around me. I could hardly believe that she was hugging me. And I was hugging her back, with tears running down my face.

"I heard what you did today for that boy. You did good, Gabby." Ernestine said, before stepping away. "I guess you're really not fake after all."

"Thanks," I said.

Ms. Baptiste looked at me and smiled. I smiled back and nodded.

Later that evening Devin picked me up and we drove down to Lenox Avenue to eat at Red Rooster in Harlem. We were greeted cheerfully when we came in. The walls were decorated with tasteful pieces of art and artifacts. It was a very welcoming environment. The music was soft and relaxing. We chose a corner table and settled in across from each other.

"I'm so happy for Caleb and his family, especially his mom," I said.

"Me too," Devin agreed.

When I examined the menu I had a hard time deciding between the blackened catfish and the oxtail stew. I finally settled on the latter while Devin had the fried chicken. And we ate and laughed and talked until our stomachs were full. Then we leaned back in our seats and just dreamed, something I hadn't done in a very long time. I had a future to look forward to and all because of God's love moving on the inside of me. All because He refused to give up on me. He had chased me every day of my life; he had run me down and finally caught me.

"Can I admit something to you?"

"Sure," Devin said.

"If this thing with Caleb hadn't come along, my time here would've been up and I would've disappeared again…"

"But everything happens for a reason."

"Well, I guess it's back to a law office for me if someone will give me a chance." I shrugged my shoulders.

"Are you kidding?" Devin's voice was strong and assuring. "After this case, you'll have your choice of jobs."

"And you Dr. Ramos, you've got bigger and brighter things ahead of you now that you've officially earned your doctorate , the school year is ending, and now that you don't have to worry about me and Caleb…"

Devin grinned. "I like worrying about you and Caleb. He's like the son I never had. And you-well I didn't realize how important you are to me until now that the case is over. I'm going to owe Simon some money but I don't care. You're very important to me."

I looked down at my plate. "Not so important. You don't need me anymore."

Devin took my hand. "But that's just it. I need you more than ever. I can't picture my life without you."

I studied Devin's face. "What are you saying?"

"I'm saying that you're so beautiful." Devin leaned forward. "And that I'm in love with you."

"Devin…I…"

"Come here," he pulled me closer to him. I could smell his woodsy scented cologne. Our noses were almost touching. And then with one slow movement he found my lips with his.

It was the most sensational thing I'd experienced in a long time. "I'm afraid…"

Devin's eyes seemed to dance under the lights. "Afraid of what?"

"I'm afraid I'm in love with you too," I said.

Devin chuckled. "I'm so glad that God answers prayer."

"Yes, Caleb is free. God is so merciful."

Devin stared at my face. "I'm not talking about that prayer. I've been praying for a wife."

"Wow." I smiled. "I really hope you find her."

"I'm sure I have." Devin kissed me again. "I promise to get the ring later on today but I don't want this special moment to pass. Will you be my wife?"

I was totally blindsided. Breathless, I tried to speak. "Devin, I…"

Devin interrupted my speech again with quick kisses. "Just say yes, please."

"Devin, I can't…"

"Wrong answer." And he kissed me again.

I started, "But we can't-"

"Wrong answer." Devin was determined to only hear a yes.

"Yes. Yes, I'll marry you. Yes," I shouted. "I think God has been trying to tell me that you're supposed to be my husband."

"Right answer. Yes!" Devin kissed me gently, then grabbed my hand and helped me to slide out of my seat.

"Where are we going?"

"I'm taking you home now," he said.

I turned around to look at him. "Did I do something wrong?"

"Not at all. In fact, you're doing everything right. That's the problem. I've disrespected too many women in the past, and I've disrespected myself too. I'm a man of God but I'm still a man at the same time if you know what I mean."

"And I'm a woman who is so grateful to God to be alive in Christ again," I said, feeling giddy.

Devin grinned. "Would you like to go ring shopping tomorrow?"

"Yep, I thought you'd never ask," I giggled.

Devin grabbed my bag and walked over to the door. He held it open for me as I walked by him. "Come on. Let's get out of here."

Devin put his arms around me in the foyer. "I can't get you out of my mind or heart."

"Me either," I agreed.

Devin's hand pressed the small of my back. "That's good to know."

"I'll have to join your church," I said.

"And we'll have to do pre-marital counseling."

"Right. Ms. Baptiste will have to help me plan an engagement party."

Devin grinned. "And I want a short engagement. I've waited too long for a wife."

I unraveled our arms, grabbed his hand and led him outside.

Devin hailed a cab as it sped towards them. "I think I'll put you in a cab."

"Why?"

"I don't trust myself to bring you home." Devin smiled. "We're going to do this right."

Holding onto his arm, I stepped into the cab, watching him the whole time.

He closed my door, tapped on the window, then blew me a kiss.

When I arrived at home, I practically floated to my room. I didn't remember what anyone said to me; it was as if they were all on mute. The only thing I heard was the Holy Spirit whispering in my ear, "*Nothing can separate you from God's love.*" Before I went to bed, I prayed an effectual fervent prayer to God for the first time in two years.

Lord, I repent for turning my back on you. Thank you Lord for what you did for Caleb today and for what you've done for me, for giving me confidence again. Thank you for never giving up on me even when I'd given up on myself. Forgive me for hating you-even if it was just for a season. I don't know why you took my husband and son away and I may never know but thank you for taking care of me and not letting me die in my misery. Thank you for being faithful. Thank you for your grace and your mercy. Thank you for bringing me back to who I really am and for giving me a second chance to be who you designed me to be.

And thanks for bringing me love again, love I thought that was dead in me. Thank you for turning me around. And thank you for turning my father around. Help him and mom on his journey to recovery. Heal him, Lord as only you can. Please also heal Ashley; let her not only live but make her whole in Jesus' name, Amen.

Oh and Lord, now I know what this thing is in me that keeps chasing me, that won't let me go, that won't let me rest in my sin, that won't let me rest in my mediocrity; it refuses to die. It's your love inside me; it's what just won't die. It's what won't die. Thank you Jesus! Amen and Amen.

If you have not yet surrendered your life to Jesus Christ,

I pray that you make that decision today.

(Romans 10:9-10)

If you or someone you know needs help:

Call the National Depression Hotline 24/7- 866-629-4564 | Free Crisis; Substance Abuse and Mental Health Administration (SAMHSA) Helpline: 1-800-662-4357. National Suicide Prevention Lifeline: 1-800-273-8255. Samaritans: 1-877-870-4673.

BOOK CLUB DISCUSSION QUESTIONS

1. Why does Gabby not like Devin when she meets him?

2. Why does Gabby refuse to leave The Home Again Women's Transitional Home?

3. Do you think Ms. Baptiste should have pushed Gabby to be more independent sooner?

4. Do you believe Gabby could have done more to help her roommate Ashley?

5. Do you think Gabby did a good job in representing Caleb on trial?

6. What, if anything, should Gabby have done differently?

7. Should Gabby have blamed her father for the death of her husband and son?

8. Do you think Gabby had a right to be angry with her mother also?

9. What could her parents have done to help Gabby?

10. Should the Home Again Women's Transitional Shelter should have done more for the ladies?

11. Why do you think Devin was drawn to Gabby?

12. Why do you think Victoria Dawson set up Caleb?

13. Why did Senator Dawson have a problem with Caleb?

14. Do you think that Devin and Gabby should get married? Why? Or why not?

15. Do you think Devin and Gabby will have children or adopt since Devin seems to have missed that in his life?

16. With only weeks left to living at the shelter, what do you think that Gabby might do next?

AUTHOR'S BIO

Ashea Goldson is a native New Yorker and a Fordham University alumna, who has called Metro Atlanta her home for over twenty years. Armed with a Bachelor's degree in communications and a Master's degree in secondary education, she is currently an English Language Arts teacher in a public high school. She is also an avid reader and supporter of literacy and the arts in her community. With her many Christian faith based novels and screenplays, she is often referred to as a "kingdom writer." Overall, she can be described as a dynamic yet relatable author, screenwriter, and entrepreneur who loves spending her quiet time with her husband, family, church family, and close friends. Follow her at Instagram @thefilmmakingfaithwriter

OTHER NOVELS BY ASHEA GOLDSON

The Lovechild

Joy Comes In The Morning

Count It All Joy

Let Joy Arise

Scorched

When Kingdom Comes

www.ingramcontent.com/pod-product-compliance
Lightning Source LLC
Chambersburg PA
CBHW060655190726
48289CB00002B/413